D0911108

Also by Kyle Stone:

The Citadel
Rituals
Fantasy Board
Fire and Ice
The Hidden Slave
MENagerie

The INITIATION *of* PB 500

Kyle Stone

The Back Room
TORONTO, CANADA

The Back Room
is an imprint of Baskerville Books.

The Initiaiton of P.B..500
© 1993 Kyle Stone
© 2001 Kyle Stone

First published 1993 by Masquerade Books, New York

National Library of Canada Cataloguing in Publication Data
Stone, Kyle
    The initiation of PB500

ISBN: 0-9686776-3-0

    1. Title

PS8587.T662815 2001   C813".6   C2001-902023-6
PR9199.3.S821615 2001

Cover photo by Norman Hatton
Cover design by Kevin Davies

Published by:
Baskerville Books
Box 19, 3561 Sheppard Avenue East
Toronto, Ontario, Canada M1T 3K8

www.baskervillebooks.com

Kyle Stone can be reached at www.kyle-stone.com

PROLOGUE

Royal! Where are you? Oh God! It hurts all over! My eyes... Everything looks underwater, rippling, indistinct. Turn on the lights! Who are these people? I'm so tired. Maybe if I sleep, I'll feel better. If the dreams don't come back. The noise...the fire...all that shouting. There was blood, smeared on that man's face when he tried to get on our Sniper. I pushed him off, my boot crunching on his cheek...Everything hurts. Royal...

Did you get all that? When it's translated maybe it will help.

If it means anything. It's probably drugged babble, like the rest. Such a pity. He's quite beautiful. All that blond hair, those intense blue eyes.

It's lucky for you we don't get to see more of them. Don't forget yourself.

Has it occurred to anyone we may be giving too high a dosage? After all, he may be strong, but he is a Terran.

It's been reduced by a third. Not that it mattered at first. When they brought him in here he was nearly gone, anyway.

The group around the bed remained attentive as they studied the naked man floating on the jets of warm air just above the mattress. They were pleased to note there was not a mark on him, now. Every gash and wound had healed, the scars been removed. The only thing remaining was the odd mark on his right buttock. That, they knew, had been put there for a reason they dimly sensed was a clue to the inner life of their patient, and they left it alone. Every hour the body was turned, gently floated to a new position. Every three hours the joints were manipulated. Twice a day healing oils were rubbed into his pale skin. He was never alone, although he only recently seemed aware of that. Every sound he made was recorded, analysed, translated, if possible. The group was very attentive. Always. Day and night.

"There you are!"
"Micah, I told you to get naked and wait."
"Well, I did, but—"
"Take off your clothes. Now."
"Yes, sir." Micah pulled the navy blue sweat shirt over his head quickly. The I.D. disks gleamed on his chest. Royal was wearing boots, tight army pants with a wide belt and nothing else. Micah felt his blood pump faster. Their games were always exciting, once Royal got into it. Micah pulled off his clothes and knelt in front of his lover. He undid the buckle and pulled the belt slowly through the loops of the pants. It was heavy in his hands and he held it a while, weighing it, spinning out the moment of anticipation. Then

6

he handed it to Royal and looked up at him.

"You want a little action? You want a little heat on your butt?"

"Yes, sir."

"'Please'."

"Please, sir."

Royal ran the belt across Micah's bare shoulders and flicked it against his back. Micah began to undo the pants quickly. Royal wasn't wearing anything underneath. Micah opened his mouth and closed his eyes. He took a deep breath— and there was nothing there. No deep, spicy smell. No scent of leather. Nothing swelling warm and living against his mouth.

"Royal! Come back! Please, sir! I'll do whatever you want. I'll do it right this time!"

Nothing but fog, and lights shining behind the fog, and those endless liquid voices....

Look. There are tears on his cheeks. How can he be suffering? Shall I increase the dosage?

No. There are other kinds of pain. Drugs can do nothing for them.

Does he guess where he is? What will happen to him soon?

How could he? There is nothing like it where he comes from, or so I understand.

He is a fine physical specimen. He will survive.

Physically, perhaps. But mentally? Will he pass the tests?

That we will find out in good time.

They were paired by the Terrafleet computer. The

memory came clear, sharp, like yesterday, although he knew they had been together for two months. It was Micah who started talking about a bonding mark. Royal didn't answer. At first.

Late one evening in their cube overlooking the station, he decided he liked the idea. He stood over Micah in his uniform with the boots that Micah kept shining and ordered him to lie face down on the bed.

"You going to do it right now?"

"It was your idea. Shut up and lie down."

"But...Maybe you better tie me up."

"Right." Royal slipped his wrists into the handcuffs and attached them to the rod along the headboard. He grabbed his ankles and tied them to the foot of the bed.

"Royal—"

"Shut up."

"Yes, sir."

Micah felt his heart beating in his throat. His palms were moist. He was getting hard. He squirmed against the sheets as Royal laid a hand on his right buttock to steady him. When the pain came, he clenched his teeth and moaned.

He's responding much better. His reflexes are fine. The skin is all healed. It's all one colour.

Lower the air jets. He can rest on the bed, now. That's it. Easy does it. Look! He's opening his eyes.

He's looking at me. He really sees me this time. Oh, I wish I could talk to him!

Save it. Stop smiling at him! He's not for us. You know that.

What a pity!

I am sub-captain Micah Starion, of the Terrafleet Corps, section 202. I am a navigator, a pilot with minor papers as a communications officer. That is all I will tell you.

You see Royal, you're not supposed to tell them any more. Of course, you know that. You've had so much more experience than me, I mean, then I. I can't see you, but I'm talking loud in case you can hear me. If you're there, please let me know. Please! I feel...weird. And I can't remember what happened. Can you? Royal?

Where am I?

ONE

omewhere at the edge of Micah's fogged consciousness, was the sound of running water. Gradually, he became aware of someone gently touching his face. He opened his eyes.

There were three of them. Three tall men with dark luminous eyes and heavy eyebrows. Although distinctly alien to him in some subtle way, the impression he received was one of caring, of kindness.

"You are Healers," he said, and they smiled, as if they understood. But then they looked at each other and once more he heard that strange liquid language slide back and forth between them. He sensed that this sound had formed a background for his dreams for some time, now. He wondered where he was and how long he had been here. Slowly he absorbed the details around him.

This was not Base Station 1, that much was obvious. He was naked, supported on jets of warm air above some sort of bed. His long blond hair was unbraided and cascaded over the pillow as if it had been arranged that way. A white light glowed above him from some unknown source. Alien symbols covered one wall. He felt the first ripple of fear.

"Where am I?" Micah looked from one dark face to another. He felt for his I.D. tags but they were not around his neck.

The Healers seemed pleased when he spoke, but they obviously had no idea what he was saying. One of them began to stroke Micah's forehead, moistening his dry lips with a soft sponge.

Flashes of memory came to Micah, fragmented pictures of violence and pain. The uprising! Flight! Could Royal be dead? He felt his eyes fill with tears at the thought of his lover and he turned away from the alien faces. I am alone, he thought. Does anyone know I am here? His eyelids fluttered and he was lost in darkness again.

Micah awoke to the realization that he had been moved. Now he was in a small room that seemed to have walls of some padded material. Muted sunlight came from the ceiling, subdued by the thick greenish glass it filtered through. In the wall at the foot of the bed, was a panel of shadowed glass he suspected might be a two way mirror.

He was still naked, but now he was lying on a narrow bed, his wrists attached with soft restraints above his head. His ankles were tied to the foot of the bed, in such a way that his legs were spread apart. He knew that he had been quite delirious at times over the past while. He pulled experimentally, trying to bring his legs together, but it was impossible. Though the material that bound him was soft, it was very strong.

Two young men came into the room, wearing the one piece white coveralls he had noted before, tight at the wrists and ankles. They were talking softly together, the liquid syllables of their strange language slipping swiftly between them. Micah flushed, painfully aware of his nakedness. As the men talked, one of them laid his hand over Micah's left nipple. Micah tensed as the hand travelled down his stomach and touched the hollow of his groin. To his horror, he felt himself respond to this casual touch. He turned his head aside, feeling the flush of embarrassment spread over his chest. The man took Micah's chin firmly between his fingers, turned his head back and smiled down at him. Then both men laughed. They undid the restraints that fastened his feet and began to articulate his knees, bending his legs back and forth, those knowing hands feeling the stretch and pull of every muscle. They repeated the procedure with his arms. Apparently satisfied, they helped him to his feet.

"At last!" Micah exclaimed, and they nodded, almost as if they could understand. He felt a little shaky, but well enough. "Where are my clothes?" The men looked at each other, puzzled. Micah gestured to their coveralls, to his own nakedness. They nodded, smiled and turned away.

"Perhaps they are taking me for a bath or a shower," Micah thought as he followed them out the door.

To his relief, there was no one in the narrow hall. It was very quiet, almost hushed. Then they came to a set of double doors and the Healers ushered him through to a different world.

Here it was warm and bright and noisy. Startled by the contrast, Micah looked around. Two burly dark men wearing bright red tunics with an emblem on the shoulder, and black pants, stepped forward at once, as if they had been waiting for the Healers. One of the men wore a black earring. He laid his large hands possessively on Micah's shoulder, feeling the muscles of his arms and thighs roughly. Incensed at this treatment, Micah broke free. The next thing he knew, his hands were caught in a grip of steel, twisted behind his back and snapped into handcuffs. It was a harsh reminder that he was a prisoner here, after all, not a patient. When Micah looked around, the Healers were gone.

The man with the black earring slapped his bare ass and gave him a push down the corridor towards the glass doors leading to the outside. Horrified, Micah realized they were taking him outdoors, naked, just as he was.

"You can't do this!" he cried, turning around.

The man peeled off his belt and hit Micah with it. The leather uncurled against his flesh, shocking him into anger and tears. But the man was not finished. With a fierce growl, he hit him again and again. Unable to shield himself with his hands fastened behind him, Micah turned away and stumbled down the corridor, the leather stinging his back and thighs and ass. These barbarians, whoever they were, probably had no treaties with his people. There was no higher authority to complain to. He would have to endure. The door opened before him and he stumbled through into the sunshine and a crowd of people.

To his surprise, no one seemed to notice the sudden appearance of a naked, bound man in their midst. His guards slipped the belt into the handcuffs and used it as a leash to pull him along through the busy crowds. Micah couldn't take in anything but the hum of activity and the fact that now and then hands touched him, prodded him. Curious hands. Rough. Male.

At last the crowds diminished and they came to a narrow gateway into a field. When one of the men pushed him roughly through the opening, Micah snapped. Instantly, he turned and pushed back. It was a mistake. At once the belt whistled through the air and tore into the flesh of his shoulders and chest and thighs. This time the man kept it up, beating him without mercy until Micah screamed and dropped to the ground in agony. The other man throw a pail of cold water over him, pulled him to his feet and shoved him into the field. They took off his cuffs.

The taller of the two men clapped his hands and made a circular motion, indicating he was to jog around the field. Shaking, Micah throw back his long hair. He was used to having it in a braid, and he found it distracting. The man with the black earring was taking a whip from a table that stood near the gate.

"Shit!" muttered Micah. He would not be whipped like an animal! The belt was bad enough. He quivered for a moment, hesitating between his pride and common sense, then turned and began to jog.

His muscles were cramped from the long convalescence and he ran much more slowly then usual, but as long as he kept going, the whip was not used. At last he heard the clap of hands that signalled he could stop. With relief he came back and dropped to the ground in exhaustion. Sweat poured from his body, dampening the fine gold hair on his chest and dripping from his arm pits. As he panted on his knees, his hands were again cuffed behind him. The brown-haired man wiped his face and produced a silver bottle with a rubber teat which he thrust into Micah's mouth. Incensed, Micah spat it out, pulling away. The man grabbed Micah's long hair and pulled his head down till his forehead was on the ground. He held it there while the other man began to hit him, his open hand making the muscles of Micah's unprotected ass dance. Micah tried to pull away from the intimate and painful contact, but it was impossible. It went on and on, the sound of the naked hand against his bare flesh loud in the air. The stinging sensation grew and grew, the heat spreading and deepening, making him more conscious of his buttocks than he had ever been before. And in spite of the torment, he knew that the hand belonged to a strong man who had him at his complete mercy, a man who thoroughly enjoyed what he was doing. Although Micah twisted against the blows until he cried out, he was dimly aware, too, of a glimmer of pleasure, sensed through the haze of his pain.

At last, to his shame and utter mortification, he came onto the grass. His hope that his tormentors would not know was shattered at once. The slapping stopped and he was jerked upright. The man who held him, reached down and pulled his slack cock, wet with his own come. Both men threw back their heads and laughed. Then the brown man produced the bottle again and forced it into Micah's mouth. Quivering with pain and humiliation, Micah sucked at the bottle. From the vaguely familiar taste, he guessed it was a kind of liquid protein, similar to what was used at the Base. As he sucked, the big man wiped his tears away. Then he felt the man's hand slide between his legs and along the crease of his ass and push its way inside him. He stiffened, but the face of the one who fed him, was warning enough. He was to allow this invasion or suffer the consequences. He could hear the rustle of clothing behind him and knew what would happen next. Panic swept through him. He was about to be raped and there was nothing he could do about it. These men had total power over him. The bottle was finished and the brown haired man forced his head down into his lap, holding Micah's ass in place for his friend. Micah felt the tip of the man's fat cock, then a sudden lunge. He screamed.

"No!"

He almost passed out from the pain. His body was drenched with sudden sweat. It seemed like forever, a lifetime of agony. Then it was over. The man who held him pulled his head up. The man who had fucked him, presented himself to be sucked. Broken and crying, Micah sucked the man clean.

How long had it been since he walked out into the sunlight of his torment? One hour? Two? It seemed like a lifetime. They led him back to the building by a different route and he followed docilely. They went into an outhouse with a stone floor. It was open on one side.

The big man who had raped him, pointed to the shower and turned on the water. The shower head was held by him, aimed at Micah's head, shoulders, genitals. He was ordered to bend over. Micah didn't care any more. He was exhausted and the hot water stung his bruised and scratched body. The man's hand directed the water up his anus, cleaning away the blood. When it was over, he stood under the radiant heat while his long hair was brushed and dried. Finally, they led him back to the main building.

This time they took him to a small room with a narrow cot equipped with the same restraints he had had before. He lay down on the bed and was manacled on his back, his legs spread apart. Even so, he fell asleep almost before they had left.

He woke up to the rough hands of the brown-haired man, who was taking off his restraints. Micah's jailer handcuffed him and led him to another room overlooking the valley. Here he was made to kneel on the floor and a large dish of stew was set in front of him. The man left. Micah was very hungry. He looked at the bowl, bent down and sniffed it. He was drooling for the wonderful rich goodness of it. But there was no way to get it except by putting his face in the plate. He pushed his knees further apart and bent over, trying to lick up the gravy and keep his balance at the same time. It was slow going. His long hair kept getting in the way, but finally he figured out how to shake it back to one side. At last he lost all dignity and pushed his face into the dish, smearing his nose and cheeks and chin in his eagerness to get a mouthful of the food. He finished off by licking the dish clean.

His jailer arrived almost at once and laughed when he saw Micah's greasy face. To Micah's shock, he leaned over and licked the gravy off his chin and nose. There was something erotic about the silken touch of this stranger's tongue against his skin. His jailer ended by kissing him, forcing his lips apart, exploring the greasy mouth inside. And Micah let him do it, wanted him to do it. He dropped his eyes when the man released him. What is happening to me? he wondered.

After that, he was taken to a large hall fitted like a gym. He was provided with an odd sort of jock strap, then, put through his paces. Apart from the fact that he was almost naked, it was much like his usual work out at home, except that it was much abbreviated, because of his convalescence. He would, he supposed, have to work his way back up to par.

This routine went on for weeks. Mornings, he went running in the field, made to go faster and faster, the whip used less and less sparingly. Then he would be forced to service one or the other of his trainers, sometimes both. Then he would be fed his bottle of protein. After that, the shower, and a nap. Lunch was always the same, stew on a plate on the floor which he was forced to eat like an animal, while his jailers watched, sometimes eating their own meal at a table on the terrace. At times, they fed him pieces of unfamiliar fruit as an extra, but for this he would have to cross the room on his knees. He learned never to touch his genitals or anus, never to pee without someone else placing his cock in one of the clear plastic bottles, always to kneel with his knees spread wide apart, so that he was continually on display for their pleasure. He found that his blond hair was endlessly fascinating to these large, dark men and they played with it constantly. His fair skin and pale pubic hair they found equally alluring. They were always touching him, running their hands over his smooth ass and the soft whiteness of his inner thighs. And although his mind rebelled, his body responded. He was often hard after their touch, and the sting of a slap brought him quickly and humiliatingly erect. It wasn't long before they played him like an instrument. Most mornings ended with Micah hard and hurting with the desire to be fucked or masturbated by their rough hands. They rarely disappointed him.

After weeks of exercise, Micah's physical condition was better than ever. His body was tanned a honey gold all over and his muscles were firm. Although the punishment never faltered, he sensed that his trainers were pleased with him and in spite of himself, this made him proud. But he reminded himself every morning that he was Micah Starion, a Nebula Warrior, and his first duty was to escape from this place of humiliation. He rarely had the chance to see much of the area they kept him in, since every day was spent going to the field, or in the gym, but he got the impression they were in some sort of fortress high on a hill. But where? It did not look like any part of Zeedon, the place he and Royal had been headed when the instruments failed. He lay awake at nights, trying to remember the star charts so that he might get some idea of where he could have crashed.

And then he would remember Royal and his heart swelled with the pain of his loss. They had had so little time together. He could still feel the sting of Royal's mark being burned into his ass as a sign of their union, only two nights before the disaster. It seemed disloyal now to regret that he had never had the chance to put any sort of mark on Royal.

It had been understood between them that this was a one way thing. It was never discussed. And now his strong, powerful lover was dead, and he was left a prisoner, alone in this foul place!

Yet in an odd way, he found his life falling into a certain comforting rhythm. And this was why he sensed a change at once when they began to treat him differently. It was not that they were any more gentle or less demanding. They still slapped him with their callused hands and pulled his hair and thrust their fingers inside him, twisting him with pain. But they no longer used the long curling whip, or beat him with the belt. They began to rub oil into his skin every afternoon. Then, one day, he noticed three new men watching his performance in the field. One of them especially caught his eye, a tall, rugged man with slate grey eyes. Unconsciously Micah put on a burst of speed, raising his head proudly and throwing out his chest. He would show them what a Nebula Warrior was capable of! A few days later, the grey-eyed man was in the gym, and the next day, he was with a group watching in the afternoon.

Then came the time when the routine changed. After his lunch, he was taken to a different room. It was similar to the shower place but there was a sort of high table in the middle and a cupboard at one side. Apprehensive at this break in routine, Micah looked around, trying to figure out the use for such a place. There was a shower here, too, he noticed, and a large tub on a raised platform.

The big man with the black earring, whom he had named Simon, after Simon Lagree, threw him into the shower stall and turned on the water full force. Micah fought to keep his balance on the stone floor, bracing himself with both hands against the glass of the walls. Then his long hair was soaped and washed. At last he was allowed under the radiant heat unit.

After that, another man appeared, whom Micah had not seen before. He was friendly with Simon, the two men talking with the ease of old acquaintance. As they talked, for the first time Micah thought he detected a name—something that sounded like Kee. This man, too, wore the red tunic and baggy pants that seemed to be some sort of uniform, but he was shorter than Simon, with an unfriendly, suspicious expression in his small black eyes every time he looked at Micah.

Kee clapped his hands and pointed to the table in the middle of the room. When Micah hesitated, Simon made a threatening move towards him, and Micah decided it would be less humiliating to climb up himself. They pulled him onto his back, attaching his ankles and wrists to the by now familiar restraints, his legs apart as usual. It was then that Micah saw the long open razor. He broke out in a cold sweat. He began to struggle, even though he knew from bitter experience that it was useless to try to break the restraints. Kee paid no attention, but began to assemble what he needed for the job at hand. When he was ready, he slapped Micah's face to get his attention, then began to spread lather on his chest. As the open blade descended, Micah froze. He did not consider himself a hairy man, but he had some hair on his chest that narrowed to a   thin line, fanning out again just above the pale bush of his pubic hair. He lay motionless as the thin steel blade swept over his body, and he held his breath in terror. Kee was obviously experienced at this job, but Micah followed the flashing blade with his eyes, until his face was pushed to one side and his cheek and jaw covered with lather. No sooner was this finished, then the whole table tilted abruptly backwards and the section between his ankles dropped away. Kee moved between his legs and grasped his balls.

"No!" cried Micah, not able to stop himself from struggling in his panic. Did they intend to make him a eunuch? "No!" he shouted. "Oh God, please! No!" But there was nothing he could do. To his surprise, Simon laid a hand on his chest. It was a gesture of reassurance, and Micah looked up at the big man gratefully.

When Kee was finished, Micah turned over. This time the procedure was less frightening, but Micah was relieved when it was over and he was lying under Simon's hands, having soothing oil rubbed into his raw skin. Simon was doing a quick, professional job this time, no lingering, exploring fingers, no pinches or sudden exploratory probes. Then leather bracelets were slapped on his ankles. They were wide, studded with silver, with a metal loop on one side. Although they were not heavy, the unaccustomed weight made Micah very aware of his legs when he moved.

Kee clapped his hands and pointed to the stool beside the table. Micah climbed down. He felt even more naked, now, with no body hair except an abbreviated bush of pubic fuzz surrounding his cock. He sat on the stool, feeling the wood rough against his ass, while his hands were cuffed behind him. Kee began to brush his long hair back from his face. Then, he took the razor and began to scrape away at Micah's hairline. Now what, Micah wondered, feeling his forehead getting higher. Long golden locks began to fall to the floor around him. Would he soon be bald? But Kee stopped, satisfied with whatever effect he had been after, and then he began to rub something into Micah's newly exposed forehead. It was a sort of cobalt blue dye, Micah noticed, close to the color of his eyes. It came to him that these people must consider this a cosmetic thing, a sort of beauty ritual, maybe. Kee added designs using a white paste and then forced the locks around his ears into a series of glass beads, which were pulled and twisted into a painful coronet around his head.

"I must look like a nightmare," Micah thought, wincing as Kee gave a final twist to his painful coiffure and pushed him off the stool so suddenly, he staggered. He would have fallen, thrown off balance by the weight of the anklets, had not Simon caught him.

Then Simon took his place on the stool and pulled Micah down across his knees. Micah could feel the push of a plastic bulb against his anus and tried to unclench his muscles, knowing from bitter experience that Simon would only use force if he didn't comply. By now, he knew enough to hold the liquid inside, and release it when Simon tapped his buttocks. What was happening? Micah worried, as he tried to concentrate on not angering the man who was handling him so casually, easily, as if he were a child.

Simon pulled him upright and the two men inspected their handy work, walking around him as if he were an object on display. They seemed satisfied with what they saw, but they were both very serious There was none of the almost playful cruelty Micah had become used to.

By now, dinner time had come and gone and still Micah was no nearer knowing what was going to happen to him. He sensed a growing tension in his two keepers that put him even more on edge. Micah's stomach gurgled loudly. Abruptly, Kee pushed him to his knees and produced the familiar, hated silver bottle. There was something so demeaning about being fed that way, having to stretch out his neck and raise his face submissively towards his handler, who often held the bottle just out of reach. But Micah was starving and he opened his mouth, sucking greedily on the rubber teat. It was unusual to be fed liquids at this time of day, and the drink had a bitter-sweet aftertaste that was also not what he was used to. Micah was so hungry he ignored the slight unpleasantness, trying to get all the liquid as quickly as possible.

A gong sounded from somewhere deep inside the huge complex. At once Kee pulled the teat from his lips. Simon straightened up and adjusted his red tunic. He picked up a blue leather collar studded with glass beads like the ones in Micah's hair and fastened it around his prisoner's neck. He attached a light chain to the collar. Kee opened the door, said something to Simon and stood aside. Simon pulled at the chain and led Micah down the hall to a large carved wooden door he had never been through before. Simon beat a rapid tattoo on the brass panel in the middle of the door, and after a moment, it opened.

Before them, three steps led down to a wall of mirrors. Micah stopped, almost falling when he caught sight of himself in the glass. Could that be him, that tanned naked barbarian with the startling blue eyes that matched the painted ribbon of blue high on his forehead? The same color was repeated in the beads that formed a headband restraining the long blond hair that fell over his shoulders. Micah's mouth fell open, but he had little time to get used to his new image before Simon pulled on his chain. A hallway stretched in two directions on either side of the mirror. Micah was led to the right. Men in brown uniforms hurried by, carrying trays full of succulent meats and gravies and platters heaped high with colorful roots and other vegetables. Micah's stomach growled again. Now he could hear noise coming from the door at the end of the hall where all the servants were coming and going. Simon led him to the door, opened it, and pulled him inside.

They were in a large courtyard, open to the skies. Automatically Micah looked up, trying to see the position of the stars, but he had no time. Simon kept pulling his chain and he was forced to look where he was going or risk the humiliation of falling. He might be a prisoner, but he was still a Nebula Warrior and he was determined to preserve as much dignity as possible.

The space was full of the sound of deep voices and laughter, the clatter of plates and cutlery, the clink of glasses. Where were the women, Micah wondered. So far, he hadn't seen any. Bright lights shone on a platform in the middle of the courtyard and it was here that Simon led him. He clapped and pointed, indicating that Micah should mount the three steps. When Micah stood in the middle of the bright circle of light, he felt Simon slip a clip on first one anklet, then the other, forcing him to stand with his legs far apart. Then he felt Simon withdraw behind him.

Micah squared his shoulders, feeling his muscles swell as he did so. He looked down on the dark, upturned faces and felt a sudden thrill of superiority. He remembered Royal's voice: "You cannot be humiliated unless you agree to it." He, Micah Starion, did not give them that right.

It was when he felt the first casual touch on his thigh that he realized there had been some sort of tranquilizer in the drink. Just as we do with animals led to the slaughter, he thought. A tall man wearing a white tunic reached up to finger Micah's left nipple. When it grew hard under his touch, the man gave it a savage twist and Micah jerked away, almost losing his balance.

"No," he told himself. "You must let them do what they want. You must not react. You must not give them that satisfaction."

But his body betrayed him. It was impossible to control the physical evidence of the pleasure their hard hands gave him, or stop the tears when they scratched and twisted and squeezed. They weighed his shaved balls in the callused palms of their hands. They were fascinated with his hair and pulled at it unmercifully, twisting it in their fingers and lifting it to their lips as if to kiss it.

And then Micah saw him, the man with the slate-grey eyes who had watched him earlier. He was bare chested, and Micah found himself wondering what he looked like under the soft suede leggings that hugged his long legs so tightly. His cold stare moved over Micah's body appraisingly. Micah could almost feel it against his sweating skin. Although the man didn't touch the prisoner, his eyes seemed to cut through to what was most private and vulnerable inside Micah's soul. Sweat trickled down his smooth well-defined chest. He wanted that man. He made himself look away .

The prisoner shivered. He was glad of the numbing effects of the drug he had been given. It was getting hard to keep his concentration, but he was aware of a change in the atmosphere of the place. Many of the men were shouting as Simon read out what sounded like a list. The clamor went on for some time, then died away.

The complete silence was alarming. Micah blinked, trying to concentrate. And suddenly, he knew. He was not a prisoner! He was a slave! Micah's head jerked back as Simon pulled him down from the platform and led him to the man with slate grey eyes. Everyone was shouting now. One word. A name?

Attlad! Attlad!

His master!

Attlad stood beside the open fire, holding a long rod. Simon pushed Micah down on his knees as Attlad raised the rod.

For a moment, their eyes met.

I am a Nebula Warrior, Micah thought. It is my duty to fight the enemy. But he didn't know who the enemy was any more. All he knew now was that he wanted Attlad, this strange, alien male, and the man wanted him. Their desire was so strong it was an almost palpable thing, vibrating in the air between them.

Then his vision cleared.

"No!" Micah lunged forward, taking Simon by surprise and pushing him off balance. Micah kicked out fiercely but the anklets throw off his aim. He fought viciously for his pride and his freedom, tearing at arms and legs with his teeth, kicking and pushing with his powerful shoulders, but the drug slowed him down, and he was not used to fighting with his hands cuffed behind him. At last he lay on the floor, held down on his side by four of the men. Screaming his rage and terror he watched in horror as Attlad lifted the branding iron and pressed it to his right bicep.

Pain shot to the center of his being. The smell of burning flesh. His brain in flames.

Micah passed out.

TWO

icah opened his eyes to darkness. He was crouched on a stone floor, his hands chained to the wall. The air was heavy and dank. When he moved, pain seared his arm and the memories rushed back. Suffering. Humiliation. He was a slave.

"No!" he shouted. "I am a Nebula Warrior!" He tried to pull away from the wall but the effort caused such agony that he passed out again.

The next time he opened his eyes, pale light struggled through a narrow crack near the ceiling. Micah's head felt wooly and he realized the effect of the drug was finally wearing off. At least it had made it possible for him to sleep.

As he peered through the gloom, looking around the small cell, he made out a huddled figure opposite him. The man was eyeing him curiously.

"So you're the Nebula Warrior," he said. His voice was low, mocking.

"You're Terran!"

"I think so. At least I used to be. I've been here so long,

sometimes I begin to wonder exactly who and what I really am. My name's Forrest Mason. Who are you?"

"Micah Starion. Why are you down here?"

"Same as you. I tried to fight them." He sighed and carefully shifted to another position.

As his eyes grew more accustomed to the light, Micah saw that his companion was younger than he was, with short dark hair and a slight wiry build. He wore the remnants of one of the brown uniforms he had seen so often on servants.

"Who are these people?" Micah asked.

"The Kudites."

"But — That's impossible! Aren't they on Darkon 3? Where the Earth Base Gamma 1 is?"

"You've got that right."

"But..." Micah pressed his forehead against the wall, trying to clear his head. "I came from there. I took off for Zeedar and there was an accident. An explosion. We crashed —"

"On Darkon 3," Forrest said. "Welcome back."

"I hadn't been long at the Base. We were so busy trying to control the riots of the colonists there, I never gave much thought to these people, the natives."

"I suspect the Terran authorities made the same mistake," Forrest remarked. "Are you a navigator?"

"Yes."

"Hallelujah! Now we have a chance!"

Micah winced in pain as his arm scraped accidentally against the wall.

"Let me see that." Forrest strained towards him in the dim light, trying to see the brand. He whistled softly. "So, you're a P.B. Well, well. That's a cut above me. The property of our great and glorious leader, too, no less."

"What does P.B. mean?"

"Personal Body Slave, a.k.a. sex object and exotic play-thing. It figures. In case you haven't noticed, they're really turned on by blond hair."

"I noticed."

There was silence in the damp cell. Micah finally cleared his throat. "You're kidding about that sex slave thing, aren't you?" he said at last.

"What do you think?"

Micah didn't answer. Looking back on his brief time here, it was all too clear that his companion was perfectly serious.

"I've been dreaming of escape for a long time," Forrest whispered after a pause. "But I don't know how to find my way by the stars. With you along, we might have a chance. Are you with me?"

"Of course. Now that I know where we are, it'll be easy."

Forrest laughed harshly. "The trick is, we have to escape first!"

"We'll make it," Micah said firmly. "There's always a way. How will we keep in touch?"

"They'll let me out eventually. Then I'll find you. Trust me, okay?"

Micah nodded. "Tell me about these people. You must know a lot after all this time."

"More than I ever wanted to, believe me." Forrest talked on and on, telling Micah everything he had managed to pick up about the Kudites. They were a lose confederacy of tribes lead by unit leaders banded together in a series of fortified complexes like this one. Their main base was called The Citadel, somewhere in the windswept rocky canyons far from the Terran base colony where Micah had been stationed. Their families stayed in this hidden city while the hunters and soldiers roamed from fort to fort, their movements based on the visions and inspirations of several of their old seers, who travelled with them and whose prophesies were listened to with great respect.

"Personally, I think they're into major drugs," Forrest volunteered, "but everyone believes it, at least on the surface."

"Are all the women back in the hidden city?"

"Most of them. But there are some all female units. I remember meeting one group a while back."

At last, the novelty of having someone to talk to, someone with concrete information, began to pall as hunger and physical needs assumed more and more importance. Finally, a soft hissing noise told Micah that his companion had given in to the call of nature.

"Sorry about that," Forrest remarked, trying to be casual.

For answer, Micah, too, gave in and gradually the acrid smell of urine was added to the damp and decay of the atmosphere. After a while, he was hardly aware of it though by nightfall, the smell was much stronger.

"God! We're going to drown in our own shit!" muttered Forrest, as the smell of excrement added its unmistakable odor to the blend.

Micah shivered, his naked body clammy with sweat and the dampness of his own urine. He had tried to move his bowels to one side, but his chain was not long enough to allow him that luxury.

By morning, his hunger had passed, but he was feeling light-headed. They were no longer talking. Forrest complained of a sore throat. Micah's arm ached dully and his hip hurt where one of the men had kicked him. All their brave talk of escaping receded into a dream and after a while, Micah slipped off into a half trance. He saw Royal's face, smiling, teasing him about something. He saw him draw his heat-rod and press it to the skin of Micah's right buttock. He woke up with a jerk. The parallel shocked him.

"Someone's coming!" Forrest hissed.

The door was flung open and the cell flooded with light. The man who stood in the doorway made a noise of disgust as he unlocked Micah's chain and dragged him outside onto a paved terrace. Micah squinted, blinded by the bright sunlight. Then the breath was knocked out of him by a blast of cold water from a hose and he fell to his hands and knees on the rough paving stones, crouching against the onslaught. The gush of water stopped as suddenly as it had begun. His guard dropped to the ground beside him and caught him in a headlock. As Micah struggled weakly, a needle pierced his backside and Micah jerked convulsively. Then the man released him, attached his chain to a post in the middle of the terrace and walked off, leaving him alone. Micah collapsed panting onto the ground.

After a while, the sun warmed his naked back and dried his hair. He lay quietly, gathering his strength, sifting through all the information Forrest had given him. There was hope, now, of a sort. At least more than there had been. But he would have to be very careful. The searing knowledge that he was slave, bought and paid for by another man, would make it even more difficult to keep from fighting back. But he would have to appear to be very docile in order to gain their confidence. Only then would there be any chance that he and Forrest would find their way to freedom.

But Micah's new-found resolve was soon put to the test. After he had been fed a bowl of the wonderful stew, Kee appeared, clapped his hands and pointed to the ground in front of him. Micah got up and went over to kneel at his feet. Kee made another gesture. Micah frowned, puzzled. Kee made the same gesture again. Micah got up and picked up his dish. He paused, looking at Kee questioningly. Kee made another gesture. This time, when Micah didn't catch on fast enough, Kee hit him with a short length of rubber. Micah flung the bowl on the floor and tried to catch the rubber club. At once, his hands were forced behind his back by the two guards, twisted high, higher until he cried out. That seemed to satisfy Kee and Micah was released. The lesson started over again.

Forrest had told him that Kee was a 'handler', as was Simon, men who were entrusted with the training and physical care of the slaves. There were many slaves like Forrest in the camp, men who did menial duties or tended the animals, but there were only a dozen or so Personal Body slaves, by Forrest's reckoning. There hadn't been any new ones for a while, which accounted for the spirited bidding for Micah. It was not easy, apparently, to find the right blend of physical and psychological characteristics. Slaves had to go through a long period of testing and training before they were fully accepted.

"They talk about it almost as if it's an honour," Micah thought now, "and yet they are training me like an animal." He was boiling with anger which he tried desperately to repress. But the combination of trying to follow the complicated signals, the rising anger at his treatment and the constant effort not to show it, was exhausting. He was thankful when at last Kee decided he had had enough and he was led back to the familiar narrow room and tied to his bed. Just before he left, Kee touched the brand burned into his shoulder. Micah stared up at him, but he could not read the odd expression on the man's closed face.

Micah found that his new routine was more taxing than before. He still ran around the field every morning, flicked by the long tongue of the whip if he slowed down the least bit, but now there was no nap. He was taken directly to the terrace and taught hand signals. Hundreds of them, it seemed. Every day Kee brought new objects and lined them up, props for his lesson. The signs for simple articles were bad enough to remember, but he found they were then combined with action signals, the hands moving faster and faster. When other men were brought in to help Kee as teachers, Micah found that each person seemed to have a signing style all his own. If his mind wandered a fraction, the stinging bite of a leather belt or a blow from a beefy hand staggered him, bringing tears of pain, anger and frustration to his eyes.

But now, he was left alone every night after his bowl of dinner, chained to the post on the terrace but alone, never the less. Eventually, one soft evening, Forrest found him there and came to join him.

"So, warrior, how's it going?" he asked, squatting beside him.

"It's hell. How do you remember all those signals?"

"We lowly menials are only taught basic commands. Personal Slaves have to be able to communicate with their masters in a more sophisticated way. Listen, I can't stay long. I've been looking for you everywhere. Are you always here after dinner?"

"So far. Don't ask me how long this will go on."

"They'll start leaving you unchained only when they think they can trust you. Please, don't fight them."

"I'm trying."

"You're my only hope, man." And Forrest glided away, blending swiftly with the shadows.

This was the first of many meetings. Micah drew comfort from these brief encounters and looked forward to his friend's visits. He would plan questions he wanted to ask him, or rehearse whole dialogues in his mind about subjects he would like to discuss. But Forrest never stayed long and he remained curiously aloof. Micah began to crave a closeness that the other continued to deny him. They never touched, not even in greeting or farewell. Forrest always sat near his friend, his arms around his knees, staring ahead of him into the shifting shadows as they talked. His voice, as he told of being sold into slavery to pay his father's debts, remained drained of emotion. He had been sold for a period of three years, but four years had gone by and no one had come to claim him.

"There's only Lucia I care about any more," he said. "She was just 18 when we got married."

"You're married?" Micah tried not to sound surprised, although in truth, the thought had never occurred to him.

"I was. A slave, of course, is not allowed to have a wife." He threw a stone into the shadows.

Micah tried to think of something to say. He shivered, suddenly aware of his nakedness in a new way.

"I've got to go." And Forrest was gone.

Micah now found a new constraint between them. He was ashamed to admit to his friend that there were aspects of his new life that he actually enjoyed; the mornings running in the field, feeling the sun on his naked body, his long hair streaming in the wind, feeling the eyes of the group of men who were often watching him. He found a secret pleasure in the knowledge that he was admired as a physical specimen, a coveted possession. Afternoons on the terrace, he was proud when his hard work at last earned him a smile or a rough pat on the head from his handlers. But he found he was often scanning the faces of the men who came to judge his progress, looking for the one that all his work was ultimately intended for, feeling more and more anxious when Attlad did not appear. All this knowledge hovered just on the edges of his consciousness, and the occasional awareness of it shamed him.

At last, one afternoon, Micah stood under the trees on the terrace, watching Kee intently as he gave him a series of linked signals that conveyed his instructions. He was so absorbed, he did not see Attlad at first, not until he had returned to Kee, bringing the bowl filled with the fruit he had asked for. When Micah finally saw the man who was his master, he stumbled and dropped the bowl, spilling its contents. At once, blows rained down on his back and thighs as he scrambled on the ground, trying to gather up the fruit. Frustrated, angry and in pain, Micah bit back his cries. When he stood up again and looked around, Attlad was gone.

That night, he dreamed of that dark face with the crown of black curls and the clear cut cheekbones. But it was the cold grey eyes that burned into him, making him writhe in his sleep and moan with unsatisfied desire. After that, Attlad began to haunt his dreams. Knowing his own shameful weakness made Micah feel awkward now with Forrest, as if he had some guilty secret that made him unfit to be Forrest's friend. They continued to talk of escape, but they would have to wait until the great Gathering, when the unit leaders and their officers rode to a special outdoor meeting place to engage in a week of war games and feasting, and Forrest wasn't sure when the next one would be.

"It depends on the visions," Forrest told him. "When it comes, everything's in confusion. It's the only time we have a chance to slip away for any period of time, unless your master chooses that moment to take you to his bed." In the shadow, Micah flushed painfully, and hoped Forrest would not notice that he was getting a hard on.

"I have to get out of here," Forrest went on. "It's been so long." His voice trailed off and they sat together in companionable silence for a while.

Forrest sighed. A moment later, Micah felt fingers stroking his hair. He said nothing, made no movement, resolved to let things take their course.

"Lucia has beautiful blond hair like this," Forrest said, his voice hoarse.

Micah leaned closer, drawn irresistibly towards the warmth and longing in the quiet voice. He realized he had been wanting this from Forrest for some time.

"She used to sit in front of the mirror and I would brush her hair for hours before we went to bed."

Down in the valley an animal cried out, the sudden noise intensifying the silence. Micah lay back on the ground, his chain jingling slightly as he adjusted himself, and gently pulled his friend down on top of him.

"Oh God!" Forrest trembled. He buried his face in Micah's hair, his lips warm against the soft skin of Micah's neck.

Micah eased down the man's pants, freeing his erection. He shifted his own hips and lifted his legs, opening himself to his friend. Forrest thrust into him eagerly, plowing deep into Micah and gritting his teeth to keep from crying out with the sudden expulsion of his great release. Then he lay on top of the blond man, breathing heavily for a moment. Micah said nothing. He sensed that Forrest had never initiated sex with a man before and was not comfortable with it now. In his heart, Micah had known this would happen. It was inevitable.

Then Forrest rolled off him and pulled up his pants. "It's late," he said. "I must go."

Micah was sitting up when a man appeared out of the shadows and pulled him to his feet. It was Kee. He unhitched the chain and dragged Micah into the building, down the hall and into the servants' quarters. He shouted something and another man jumped to his feet and rolled a barrel onto its side. Kee threw Micah down over the barrel, his head hanging down, blond hair sweeping the ground, his legs splayed wide, and examined his anus. Micah gritted his teeth, knowing the telltale signs would give him away. Had they been watching from the shadows?

A leather belt whistled through the air and cut into his buttocks. Micah groaned. He knew he would be punished severely. He had committed the cardinal sin. He had forgotten for a moment that every part of him belonged to Attlad now. Micah was not free to give himself to anyone. He had no private parts. Until he had passed all the tests, he was public property, and they would remind him of that right now. The blows went on and on, until Micah thought he could bear it no more. His face was wet with traitorous tears. Then the cheeks of his ass were pulled wide apart and a thick cock was shoved into him. He moaned, reaching out blindly to steady himself. The barrel rocked back and forth as the man thrust into him. The wine inside sloshed about. Micah felt sick to his stomach. Then another man raped him, hard and fast. Then another. Micah cried out in spite of himself and his torment continued. Over and over. Micah was no longer capable of thinking. His mind swam with pain and humiliation. Just when he thought the punishment was over, his skin was assaulted once again with the belt or a whip. And then it started again. He lost track of time. When he threw up, they finally pulled him upright and tied his hands to the wall above his head. Then, at last, it was over. They had tired of their sport. Simon untied him and led him to his room.

The big man pushed him onto his stomach and tied his hands and feet. Then he rubbed ointment on his bruised and flaming buttocks and thighs and calves while Micah tried to control his breathing. Just before he left, Simon turned and laid a hand on Micah's cheek in a caress. And that was what broke him. That one act of kindness was too much and Micah burst into noisy tears.

"I'm sorry!" he cried, forgetting that Simon could not understand the words. "I won't do it again!"

Simon patted his face and smiled down at him. He raised his right hand to cut the air with his words. "You are beautiful," the gestures said, "but you are a slave. Do not forget that." Then Micah was left alone, sobbing in the darkness.

Micah was not always sure about the passage of time. His days slid by, patterned in a routine of pain and physical exercise and long hours of lessons in signing. Forrest did not return to the terrace and at first Micah worried that he, too, had been punished. Then he caught sight of him one day, carrying trays in the corridor and although he gave no sign, Micah was relieved.

It wasn't until several weeks later that Attlad showed up again on the terrace. This time he clapped his hands and Micah sprang to attention, his eyes riveted on his master. Attlad's hands moved smoothly, his gestures quicker and more concentrated than he was used to. Desperately Micah watched the strong brown hands cutting the air, knowing this man had total power over him. But most of all, he felt consumed by his deep longing to prove his worth to Attlad, to gain some acknowledgement of the efforts Micah had been making to learn to communicate with him. But the movements were too fast, too abbreviated. Micah hesitated, glanced at Kee for guidance and lost his place. In confusion he knelt in front of Attlad, and raised his own hands, trying to ask for another chance. Attlad towered above him, his hands now motionless at his sides. Micah braced himself, knowing that now the punishment would come. He would be beaten, punched, tied to the tree, perhaps suspended from its lowest branch as he had been last week and left to the agony of his own weight pulling on his painfully stretched arms.

Nothing happened.

He raised his eyes fearfully and met the utter contempt in the grey eyes that looked at him as if he were nothing but a part of the inanimate landscape. Then Attlad turned on his heel and walked away, talking over his shoulder to the man who was his second-in-command who walked, as always, at his side.

The beating given him by Kee was nothing compared to the laceration of that look, so totally devoid of interest.

"Just you wait!" Micah muttered, clenching his teeth. He thought once again of Forrest and their pact to escape. "When you want me, I won't be here!"

icah sat on the terrace and watched the sun sink into a bloody sea through the tangle of trees below him. It was always warm here, even in the evening, and although he was, as usual, naked, he felt no chill in the air. His handlers no longer chained him up when they went for their evening meal. After all, where could he go, a naked man with Attlad's brand on his arm? Anyone in the complex would be delighted to turn him in, should he try to escape in such an obvious manner.

"Chento."

"Forrest!" Micah jumped to his feet, delighted to hear Forrest's voice again. They had not talked since the evening they had made love and Micah had been so severely punished. He started towards his friend, smiling broadly. But Forrest backed away. Micah stopped. "What's the matter?"

"The matter? Why should anything be the matter in this best of all possible worlds?" Forrest sat down on a stool and picked up a piece of fruit left over from Micah's dinner.

Micah hesitated, chilled by the unfamiliar bitterness in his friend's voice that seemed directed at him. He straddled a chair, trying to conceal his genitals. He was angry that Forrest made him feel this way. "I thought we were friends," he said.

"Friendship is a luxury slaves can't afford," Forrest answered, biting into the fruit. "I'm not the enemy."

"What did you call me just now? I've heard it before."

"Chento. Of course you've heard it before. It's your name. Strictly speaking, of course, it's not a name, but a number. 500, to be exact. It's what they call you. It's even part of your tattoo."

Micah said nothing. His anger and confusion were growing as the sharp unfeeling words cut into him. They were so unexpected from this quarter he didn't know how to react.

"It's getting nearer to the Gathering," Forrest said, throwing the core over the edge of the terrace. "Still interested in getting away? Or are you beginning to enjoy all the attention?"

"I'm getting the strong feeling you don't want to go anywhere with me," Micah said.

"We can't always choose in this world."

Micah turned away. Forrest was the only one he could talk to in his own language in this place, apart from the translator, Nex, whom he rarely saw and couldn't trust anyway. But could he trust Forrest? Had that last scene together been some kind of a set-up? Was it just another one of the tests Forrest had warned about in their earlier, more friendly talks?

Forrest got to his feet and hesitated a moment, before coming over to Micah. "Look, I'm sorry to take it all out on you like this. It's been pretty rough lately, okay?"

Micah wanted to say, do you think it's been easy for

me? but he bit back the words and took Forrest's out-
stretched hand instead. "I still want to escape," he said.
"Just tell me when."

"Don't worry. I'll let you know."

"You can count on me," Micah said.

The next day, when Micah was taken to the field,
there were two horses tethered by the gate. Micah looked
up at them warily. He was a technocrat. He had been
trained to control machines. Animals frightened him, not
because he was timid, but because he was not sure how to
control a creature with a will of its own. He had never been
close to animals and these two looked enormous to him.
They rolled their eyes when they looked at him and snorted as if angry.

Simon and Kee and several men he didn't know stood
about talking together. Micah steeled himself for some new
humiliation, but he was not expecting what happened. The
tallest of the men suddenly grabbed him and flung him over
the horse's back, as if he were a sack of vegetables. His head
hung down on one side, his long hair sweeping the ground,
his legs on the other. He felt his ankles being bound
together, then his hands. One of the men leapt up on the
horse's back and they cantered off.

Micah was terrified. In spite of the ignominious position, he was glad to feel the man's hand on his bare buttocks. At least it gave him some small sense of security. But
as the horse moved faster and faster, he felt a scream of terror rising in his throat and at last he heard his own voice,
crying out in fear. The horse slowed down and stopped and
he heard the men laughing. With a parting slap to his bare
ass, the man jumped down and the horse began to move.
Micah could see the man's feet under the horse's belly as he

walked along, presumably leading the great beast around the field while Micah tried to get a feel for the rhythm of the animal under him so that he could balance himself. He found, however that he had almost no control. No matter how much he clenched and unclenched his muscles, there was little he could do to control his fate. The ground tilted by, his hair obscuring any view but what he could see upside down under the horse's belly. When he realized he was not going to fall, his fear retreated a little and he found it easier to concentrate. He was relieved when the horse stopped again and he was pulled off.

They gave him a drink and untied his feet. This time they threw one leg over the horse's back and the animal started off again. Micah leaned forward, his bound hands in the horse's coarse mane, his knees tightly clenched around the animals heaving sides. As it moved, its back slapped against his bare ass and the coarse horse hide rubbed his naked thighs, but all Micah was aware of was the field jolting by and the harsh voices of the men laughing and shouting to each other. This time, the horse stopped suddenly and he lost his balance and fell heavily to the ground. This caused great pain to him and great merriment to the onlookers. Simon lifted him up and released his hands. At least it would now be easier to balance, Micah thought as they hoisted him on the accursed creature's back once again. The horse snorted as if even less pleased than Micah, and they started off again. One of the men stood in the middle of the field, holding the horse by a long lead and touched it's flank with a whip. Now and then the whip flicked Micah's buttocks or thighs and he knew it was no accident. After what seemed hours, he began to feel more confident. He fell off several more times, but little by little he began to loose his unreasoning fear. But his muscles ached as never before by the time they allowed him to rest and he sank down gratefully on the ground.

As he knelt on the grass, soaked in sweat, bruised and scratched from his falls, Kee brought the silver bottle and gave him the signal to go on all fours. Wearily he obeyed, submitting without a murmur as one of the handlers began to rub down his body as if he were an animal, pushing his legs wider apart so he could touch the raw inner thighs. Micah stretched his neck towards Kee, sucking obediently at the cool rubber teat, not even stopping as his anus was invaded by a gloved hand.

The afternoon wore on, but by the end, Micah was riding quite well, steering the animal around the ring in figure eights with his knees. But his ass was raw and sore and his genitals were bruised from being constantly slapped against the horse's back. He was totally exhausted when they finally let him slide to the ground, too tired to feel any embarrassment as he bent his knees and urinated in the grass, hands behind his back.

That evening, after his dinner on the terrace, Simon took him to his room and gave him a rub down. The big man's hands moved over him gently, rubbing in the cooling ointment. It was all so wonderfully soothing, Micah almost drifted off. The sharp slap against his sore buttocks brought him back at once. His eyes snapped open and he saw Attlad looking down at him. At once he slipped off the bed and onto his knees before him. His master raised his chin and gazed down at him, the grey eyes unreadable. Then he gestured to Simon who hoisted him back on the bed and bound his ankles and wrists. Attlad took a small wand from his belt. When he twisted the handle, it made a high pitched hum and Micah tensed with fear. Simon held his right buttock and Attlad passed the wand close to his skin. Micah cried out in spite of himself when the pain bit into him. Royal's mark! They were taking it away! Once again the pain burned into him. He tried to struggle but it was too late. They were erasing his history, his past. Another piece of his identity, gone in a few waves of burning pain. It was over in less than a minute and the men went out, leaving him alone to his suffering and the darkness.

In the next few weeks, the riding sessions in the field were repeated day after day. The tender skin of his inner thighs and buttocks were constantly rubbed raw and bleeding but Micah was at last beginning to have a sense of controlling the animal under him. He would always hate riding, he knew, but at least the unreasoning fear of the unknown was gone. Micah felt that he had passed another test.

Every evening he was washed and rubbed down by Simon, whose hands were becoming almost loving in their caresses. Micah relaxed with him, letting himself drift off now and then, confident that Simon would not torment him.

After one of these sessions, Micah became aware that Simon was taking extra care with him. He brushed Micah's long hair and rubbed scented oil over his buttocks and between his legs. He put a blue leather collar around his neck and blue leather bracelets on his wrists and ankles.

"Why?" Micah asked with his hands.

"Your master wants you," Simon replied. "He is in the Dining Hall. He wishes to reward some of the men."

"Reward?" Micah knew the sign, but the word in this context frightened him. But he couldn't get any more information out of Simon, who refused to make any more signs. Simon snapped the chain onto his collar and led Micah down to the Dining Hall.

The soldiers and their leaders had been eating and drinking for some time. The faces of many of the men they passed were flushed with wine. Micah was relieved to reach Attlad and he knelt obediently at his feet, his knees spread wide as always. He would have liked to look around the room but was afraid he might miss some sign from his master's hand. Attlad fed him tidbits from his own plate and held out the goblet of wine for him to drink, laughing when he poured too fast and the red liquid spilled over Micah's chin and ran down onto his smooth chest.

When the food was taken away and more wine was brought, Micah caught sight of Forrest hurrying back and forth carrying the heavy baskets filled with wine bottles. He started when Attlad clapped his hands and ordered him onto the table.

"On your back," his master signaled. "Spread your legs for my friends."

It's another test, Micah thought, scrambling to obey. He wanted to close his eyes to shut out the sight of the great flush-faced sweating man over him, but he was afraid of missing a signal from his master. The man opened his pants, releasing his swollen cock, and pulled Micah to a more convenient position. He plunged into him without warning, riding Micah hard, his thick cock thrusting deep. Micah's eyes filled with tears as the edge of the table cut into him. The man sitting beside the one fucking him, reached over and pulled at Micah's right nipple, twisting it in his fingers and squeezing it between his nails. Sweat broke out on Micah's body and he clenched his hands. Other men were pulling at his hair, feeling the muscles in his arms. When the man came, he collapsed back onto his chair, and Micah was pulled into position by another man who had been waiting his turn. This man forced Micah's legs up over his shoulder and thrust deep inside him. Micah moaned and twisted, his hands opening and closing convulsively, but he forced himself to remain passive, submissive to the soldiers thrusting desire, trying to ride out the pain. Although he gritted his teeth, he couldn't stop the muted cries.

When this onslaught was over, Attlad pulled his slave back to him and poured wine down his parched throat. The red liquid flowed over his face and neck and chest, but Micah gulped what he could. Then Attlad forced his head down onto his lap and held him there firmly while Micah's legs were kicked wide apart and an unseen man drove his swollen cock up Micah's ass. Micah clung to his master, taking comfort in the muscular arms that held him and the thighs that felt rock hard under his weight as he was pushed against him repeatedly. He smothered his cries of pain in his master's crotch until at last, Attlad called a halt to his torture. He held Micah's red, tear-stained face between his rough hands and kissed his swollen, wine-stained lips. Then he pushed him down to squat between his legs, where Micah stayed, afraid to move. The slave's eyes anxiously watched Attlad's every move, while his master laughed and talked and played with Micah's long hair.

"Chento," said Attlad, patting his cheek. "Chento."

"Master." Micah made the sign twice. Exhausted and aching, he laid his head against his master's knee and finally closed his eyes.

When at last Kee came to take him away, Micah found it painful to walk. As he made his way through the emptying hall on a leash behind his handler, he carried the feeling of Attlad's parting kiss on his lips and knew that at last he had pleased his master. He had submitted totally to Attlad's will. He had opened himself without holding back to everyone his master gave him to. He knew he had passed another test.

The next day, Micah had a feeling that something was about to happen. He could sense a mounting excitement in the air, and realized that last night had been a kind of celebration, a prelude. The Gathering, at last! But his routine went on as usual until the middle of the afternoon. Then he was taken to his room and presented with a tunic and leggings.

"Put them on," Kee signalled without expression. He watched as Micah slipped the tunic over his head. The front was cut low, exposing his nipples, but it was long enough to cover his genitals, at least. As he stepped into the pants, he realized they weren't leggings at all, but chaps, open both front and back. All it would do was protect his legs, while his cock and ass were fully visible under the tunic. Somehow, this slight covering made him feel more exposed than when he had been naked, and he was embarrassed to see Kee watching him.

He was taken back to the field which was now filled with horses and riders, and he was tied beside a beautiful, huge black stallion, which bore Attlad's symbol on his hide, just as Micah did. All the riders were officers in Attlad's service and they sat their horses easily, waiting for their leader.

When Attlad arrived, he sprang easily into the saddle and waited impatiently while Micah was hoisted up in front of him. Then he gave the signal and the long column of horsemen moved off, out of the field and down the long hill into the woods.

At first, the road was wide and obviously much travelled. Attlad amused himself by resting his hand on Micah's genitals under the tunic. He caressed and squeezed and pulled at the stiff cock until it ached, tormenting Micah into the occasional moan, which he could not suppress. Sometimes Attlad's hand would withdraw briefly, but it was only to pull at one or other of Micah's taut nipples, displayed so plainly just above the neckline of the tunic.

After a while, Attlad pulled the tunic up and tucked it into Micah's belt, so that the red tip of his slave's dark bursting cock stood up plainly for all to see. And all the time, he talked and laughed with the men who rode beside him, as if totally unaware of Micah and the desperate pain he was causing him.

When a wineskin was passed around, Attlad squirted a generous portion into Micah's mouth, much of which spilled onto his chest. Then his hands dropped back to his gentle torment, drawing another moan of pained desire from Micah.

Three of his captains were riding beside Attlad when Micah realized his master had decided to bring him to orgasm. Micah looked at him beseechingly, but Attlad paid no attention. Micah suffered agonizing humiliation as he felt the first wave of his release roll over him. In spite of every effort, he couldn't stop a deep moan of pleasure and he arched back against his master's hard body, shuddering and gasping, red faced with shame as his come shot over the horse's neck. Shaking, he dug his fingers into the horse's mane. The men were all laughing, Attlad loudest of all as he held his shuddering slave against him to keep him from falling. At last, Micah's reddened and abused cock was slack.

They took a break to rest the horses. Micah knelt beside his master, eating grapes from his hand and taking off his tunic when he was ordered to. At once he felt even more exposed in the chaps, but there was nothing he could do. When it was time to start again, Attlad decided that Micah was to ride alone. A smaller horse was brought forward and attached to Attlad's with a leather lead. Micah was hoisted onto the horse's back and his hands bound behind him. Then Attlad ordered him to bend over the horse's neck and raise his buttocks, while he shoved a leather dildo up his slave's ass. Red faced with shame, Micah stared ahead of him, knowing what was going to happen. Every jolt of the horse sent the phallus deep inside him and he was erect again at once, unable to relieve his misery. Now he knew why Attlad had ordered him to take off the tunic. He wanted to be able to see his slave's aching state of desire at a glance.

Micah had no idea how long the ride would be. For him, every step was misery. Just riding with his hands tied behind him was bad enough, taking all his concentration, without any added distraction. From time to time, Attlad would glance at him, at his strained, tear stained face and straight back, his erect and bursting cock, and would smile, pleased. Micah gritted his teeth and wondered how long this test would go on.

At the next stopover, Attlad took his slave away from the others into the woods. Even though he was not tied, now, Micah felt completely controlled by Attlad's will. He still had the phallus up his ass, clenched with his muscles so it would not come out. When they came to a tree with a branch just above Micah's head, they stopped and Attlad removed the phallus. He ordered Micah to reach up and hang onto the branch. When he did so, Attlad pushed his legs far apart and began to fuck him, with deep, slow thrusts, impaling Micah on his thick cock. Micah cried out, working his hips and clenching his muscles to bring Attlad even deeper inside. Attlad reached around his waist and began to masturbate him, his hand rough and possessive, and Micah shouted as they came almost at the same time. On his master's signal, he dropped from the branch and squatted on the ground, letting Attlad's juices drain out of him. Before he led him back to the horses, Attlad kissed him fiercely, biting at his lips until they bruised.

The rest of the way, Micah rode alone, his horse tethered to his master's great stallion. As they rode through the afternoon sunshine, he watched his master's back and the powerful haunches of the black horse. He wore his tunic again and his hands were unbound. But every jolt of the horse was sexual to him now, in spite of what his mind told him. And he knew his lips carried the visible scars of his master's passion just as his sex was still half erect from his master's touch. And his body shivered and thrilled with the heat of the animal shifting under him and his ass still felt stretched, filled with his master's cock.

FOUR

I t was late afternoon when they arrived at the encampment. The vast open area was surrounded on three sides by rocky cliffs where the low lying sun gleamed on the tips of weapons and metal helmets. One section was filled with colorful tents with the insignia of the many different leaders and chieftains flying from the center poles. Nearby, horses were tethered and in another spot, men in the brown uniforms of servants were setting up trestle tables and preparing great fires laid in pits dug deep in the ground.

As Attlad rode into the camp at the head of his unit, his slave on the horse behind him, the men already there let out a cheer that echoed around the rocks and came back to them again. Attlad was evidently a popular leader, even amongst those who did not serve under him.

They rode to the largest tent, made of green and black silk with Attlad's dragon pennant flying from its flagpole, and dismounted. Micah had been a slave for months now, but the scene around him, alien and primitive though it was, aroused bitter memories of his past as a soldier. While the leader talked to his men, Micah stood tense by his side, waiting for instructions. Outwardly attentive, his agile mind worked on the possibilities for escape presented by the sprawling encampment and the river he saw glinting in the distance.

At last Attlad turned to him. "Take off your pants," he signed abruptly.

Micah gritted his teeth and obeyed. It didn't really surprise him. But when Attlad ordered him to take two pails and get water for the horses from the river, he felt a hot wave of rebellion shoot through him and he raised his head. He was a warrior! He might be a slave, a toy for Attlad's pleasure, but he was not a menial servant! He stared back at the man defiantly. The cold grey eyes locked into his and held them.

"You do not obey?" Attlad's hands sliced the air, as clear as any spoken words.

Micah trembled with anger, but the task offered a valuable opportunity to reconnoiter, a chance that was far more important than his pride. Setting his jaw, he went over to pick up the wooden buckets that stood by the hitching post.

He could see the silver thread of the river down through the trees. He followed the path away from the crowds in the tent area until the sound of their voices grew distant and he was alone. He slowed down, beginning to enjoy the peace and beauty of the scene, the feel of the cool earth against his bare feet. The path slanted down to the water abruptly and Micah waded into the stream with pleasure. Oh how he would love to swim here, soothing his aching bones and hot skin in the green fast running water, but he was afraid to anger his master, who would see his wet hair and know at once he had been enjoying himself and not following orders. Micah knelt in the water, letting it caress his thighs and buttocks as he filled the pails. The river sang around him, bursting into a small waterfall just before it rounded the bend out of sight. Long-legged birds wadded along the opposite shore, their inquisitive heads cocked to one side as they regarded him with interest. When he began to worry that he might be missed, he carried the pails up the bank and started regretfully along the path back the way he had come.

Suddenly a group of boys blocked his way. Micah stood still and looked at them warily. One of them carried a bow. Several others held stout sticks. They stopped too and looked Micah up and down, laughing and giggling like children. One of them darted close and gave his hair a hard yank, almost as if to test if it were real. Another boy reached out with his stick and slapped Micah's cock. Micah yelped in pain and jumped back, spilling some of the water. He put down the buckets and took another step away from the boys, who now began to circle him, their eyes bright with cruelty. It would be easy to scatter them if he could fight as he had been taught, Micah thought, but they saw him as a slave. How was he expected to react in this situation? A stick jabbing at his balls decided the issue and Micah grabbed the stick out of the boy's hand and dropped into a crouch. The boys backed away, confused by this response from a slave. Then the one with the bow clapped his hands and made the signal to kneel.

"Not to you!" muttered Micah.

The boy began to shout at him. The others joined in and the path was soon ringing with their anger. Micah backed up against a tree, determined to defend himself, but not purposefully hurt any of them. He gave a hoarse, guttural growl, which startled his tormentors as it was meant to do. Micah was just thinking that he might come out of this all right, when Attlad and two of his men arrived. Micah prudently dropped the stick. For a moment it seemed that everyone was talking at once.

When Attlad looked at him, Micah signed quickly: "They attacked me."

Attlad pointed to the ground, his hands eloquent in their command.

Seething, Micah dropped to all fours, trying not to see the glint of triumph in the boys' eyes. Attlad and his two companions sat down on a fallen tree and watched as the boys walked around Micah, poking him between the legs, slapping at his cock and pulling his fascinating blond hair. The young leader paused behind him and spread his buttocks. Micah's face flushed with indignation, but Attlad only laughed and seemed to be actually encouraging the boy with his explorations. Next, Micah felt the tip of the boy's penis pushing inside him. To his horror, one of the others now stood in front of him, opening his pants. Micah drew back and looked frantically at his master.

"Suck him!" Attlad ordered, his hands angry and decisive.

Micah saw the youngster's hands tremble as he took out his cock and presented himself to be sucked. It took every once of Micah's self control to take the boy in his mouth gently and pull at him, careful not to let his teeth harm him. And all the time he sucked the young one, all the time the leader pumped into his ass until he came, Micah's own arousal was painfully obvious. Micah drained the youngster and let him go. He kept his eyes on the ground and the others whooped and hollered around him. Two more took the places of the first pair and once again Micah took the slender boy cock deep in his throat and drank it, savoring its sweetness, while the boy's friend thrust into his anus. It was quickly over and the youngsters raced off through the trees, soon followed by the two men.

Attlad and Micah remained alone. Micah stayed where

he was, afraid to look at his master. He could feel the anger. When he heard the sharp clap of his hands, he looked up, got to his feet and walked to the tree Attlad was pointing to. He embraced the trunk of the tree and Attlad kicked his feet far back, making him bend far down, and spread his legs wide. Then he drew off his belt and began to beat his slave. Tears soon washed Micah's face as the boys' warm cum dripped down his legs. The silence of the woods was filled with the slave's labored breathing. He began to moan with the pain, trying to avoid the lash of the leather against his stinging thighs. He could feel the welts rising on his ass, the red lines springing along his back and the backs of his legs. At last he wept noisily, his eyes blinded with his tears. But Attlad didn't stop until Micah was on his knees, all dignity gone, praying him for mercy. Attlad put his belt back on and threw a pail of water over Micah.

"Chento, you needed punishment."

"Yes, master." Micah's hands trembled as he made the signs.

"When will you learn that you have no will? No choice?"

"Please, master! I am sorry!"

"Stand up."

Micah struggled to his feet. Attlad wiped his slave's flaming face with his shirt sleeve and dropped his hand to Micah's erect cock. He stood there for a moment, stroking it until Micah whimpered in spite of himself.

"Please," Micah whispered, pushing his hips forward, trying to get some relief.

Attlad smiled and pointed to a moss covered tree stump. Micah stared at the sign he made, not sure he had read the words right. Attlad repeated them. "Fuck yourself."

Micah sank to his knees in front of the tree stump and rubbed his swollen cock against the soft bark, his hands braced on the rock behind. Attlad watched as Micah lost all dignity, all grace, and began to pump his hips up and down, uttering small moans until at last he came, his semen spurting over the mossy stump that was now half destroyed by his frenzied efforts. Micah was crying softly, kneeling on the ground with his shrunken penis red and raw from the violence he had just done to it. I am nothing but an animal in heat, he thought miserably, and he wiped his hands against his stinging thighs.

At last, he looked up through his tears to see Attlad pointing to the pails. Wearily, Micah got to his feet, filled both pails again and followed his master.

It was getting dark by the time Micah reached the camp and Kee took him away to a hut on the edge of the circle of tents.

"I will prepare you for the ceremony," Kee signed, looking at him with distaste.

"What ceremony?" Micah asked, his hands trembling. "What will I have to do?"

"Whatever you are told to do. Your master will display you to the men. You will show every part of you for their enjoyment. I tie back your hair so they can see your pretty face all the time, as well as your pretty cock and ass." He grinned. Micah winced as Kee slapped his sore penis. "All want to see and touch the leader's new toy for the last time. After tonight, if he gives you the rings, no one can touch you but your master."

Micah lay on his back and watched Kee's moving hands avidly, trying to understand what he was being told. The man motioned for Simon to pour water over Micah and rub him down. His hands kept moving and Micah tried to follow.

"When you are clean and sweet smelling, your master will come and lead you to the feast where you will be displayed while we eat. If he is pleased, he will put his mark on you. Understand?"

Micah nodded. He knew this was to be a further test and pride made him hope he would acquit himself well. He raised his hands to ask a question, but Kee turned on his heel and left the hut.

Simon was gentle with him, obviously understanding something of the agony he had been through. He rubbed oils and ointment into his wounds until the sting was dulled and the pain had retreated. Gently he washed the limp penis and rubbed more oils into it until it began to stir into life. The man smiled faintly and Micah blushed and turned his head away. Then he produced the silver bottle and held it to Micah's lips. This time he recognized the bittersweet taste of the drug and sucked it greedily, thanking the man with his eyes. He sensed that this was not a part of the ritual but something Simon had added on his own initiative, and Micah was thankful.

Micah was left to rest for a while, drifting in and out of a light sleep. When he sensed someone beside him, he opened his eyes and gasped. Forrest was standing there, looking down at him in the dimness.

"It's almost time," Forrest whispered. "Tonight is the feast. By tomorrow, they'll all be hungover, but they'll feast again anyway, at noon, waiting for the old man to have his vision."

"What old man? What vision?"

"Attlad's father. That's what this is all about, supposedly. They're praying for the vision even as we speak. But what they're thinking of is your golden locks and pretty thighs and swollen cock that will soon be presented to them."

"Forrest —"

"Listen. By tomorrow at dusk, they'll all be out of it. Attlad will be busy with his prayers and consultations. Half the camp will be breaking up. Some will have left. Some will be sleeping it off. Discipline breaks down and people get slack. Meet me by the river. Do you know where the water fall is?"

Micah felt his face flush as he remembered the place of his abject degradation. Knowing the way people talked, he suspected Forrest had already heard of his encounter with the boys. He nodded his head.

"I will wait for you in the thicket with a brown uniform like mine. Can I count on you?"

"Of course!" Micah was angry at his lack of trust.

"Micah, you still don't understand, do you? After tonight, you may be one of them."

"Impossible! I am a Nebula Warrior."

"So you say," Forrest murmured. "I will be in the thicket." Before Micah could say anything else, he disappeared.

Micah lay in the dimness, thinking about what Forrest had said. He was troubled by the sudden realization that he could no longer remember Royal's face. It was vague to him, a pale blur. The man he had loved, who had burned his mark into his ass, was fading from his mind, along with his old life, his warrior training, his pride and strength of purpose. Forrest was right. There was danger in staying here too long! He had to escape before it was too late!

He was startled by the sudden entrance of Kee, who set about briskly getting him ready for the evening. His hair was twisted out of sight under a tight leather cap. His anus was cleaned, his pubic hair brushed and trimmed. A wide leather collar with large blue and silver spikes was fastened around his neck and strong leather bracelets secured to his ankles and wrists. A black line was painted on the high part of the forehead.

When Attlad strode into the hut, he seemed to fill the small space with his massive size. Kee stepped back at once.

Micah stood up, waiting for the hand signal to tell him what to do. Instead, Attlad took a small bottle from the pouch at his waist and pulled out the stopper. He dabbed the red-brown liquid on Micah's hard nipples and the underside of his penis. Then he picked up the bottle of wine on the table and took a long drink. He pulled Micah's face to his and kissed him hard. When Micah opened his mouth to the unexpected caress, the warm liquid from Attlad's mouth flowed into his, almost gagging him with the strong, heavy sweetness of the wine. Micah swallowed, his lips clinging to Attlad's a moment longer. Then his master clipped a leash to his slave's collar and led him outside.

By this time it was dark. Great flaring torches were everywhere, casting an eerie light over the camp. From the meadow below came the sound of a large group of men talking and laughing together. Attlad leapt easily onto his mount and twisted the leash around his hand. After a moment, they started off at a brisk trot, Micah beside him, his arms cuffed behind him, his head held high.

Attlad quickly gathered speed until Micah was running fast, afraid of losing his balance and being dragged ignominiously into the gathering. A cheer went up as they appeared at the amphitheater where the trestle tables were set up. Attlad touched his horse into a gallop and Micah broke into a frantic pace, determined to keep up. They stopped at a stone platform at the other end of the area, lit by a circle of torches. Chains hung from a scaffold high above them and a fire flared down below.

Attlad turned his horse to face the assembly and began to make a speech, sitting at ease on his nervously prancing horse. Micah was hoisted up onto the stone platform where he stood catching his breath and waiting for a signal from his master.

When it came, it shocked him. "Display yourself," Attlad's

hands said.

Micah glanced about frantically trying to find a way out. But Attlad flicked his stinging whip across Micah's ass. In a reflex action, he thrust his hips forward, bending his knees.

"More," Attlad commanded, raising his whip.

Micah pumped back and forth, trying not to feel the shame caused by his lewd gestures, as the crowd hooted with pleasure. Then Attlad told him to turn around and show them the rest. "Open yourself for them," he ordered. Obediently, Micah bent down and parted the cheeks of his ass. Attlad reached over and pushed his head lower, forcing his ass higher, his legs wider apart, and Micah closed his eyes, trying not to hear the jeers of the men.

When he was allowed to straighten up, Kee attached the chains to the bracelets on his ankles and wrists. Then Kee gave a signal and the chains tightened, raising him into the air. A shout went up from the crowd as the slave was hoisted above them by his arms. Micah gritted his teeth. Slowly his legs were raised until his feet were on a level with his hands, and his body was bent double like an animal suspended on a spit for roasting. The men laughed as they ate and drank, looking up at the brightly lit platform where their leader's latest toy hung on display for their enjoyment.

The chains moved gently, swinging back and forth and creaking slightly in the breeze. Micah tried to stay utterly still, cutting down on the sickening movement, but this was useless. Every few minutes, the length of the chains was altered, so that at times he was stretched almost taut, the manacles on his wrists and ankles cutting into his skin. Then the chains would lengthen and move close together so that his ass was split wide open and he was utterly exposed to their curious scrutiny. Then again he was abruptly lowered, his feet swung around and up again, so that he hung facing the crowd, his arms pulled back painfully behind him, his cock pointing down towards the appreciative audience.

On and on, the men feasted and drank and shouted below him. Some of them climbed up on the tables, trying to touch him with their sweaty hands. Time ceased for Micah as he struggled to cope with his excruciating torment. Each new position increased his awareness of the threshold of his own pain. By the time he was lowered to the stone platform and unshackled, he could hardly stand. The tortured muscles of his arms and thighs screamed in protest. A frenzy of shouting and hand waving broke out below him, but he couldn't make out what was happening as he was taken to his master's side.

Attlad was making another speech which his audience seemed to appreciate a great deal. He finished by holding up both hands, his fingers spread out. Ten. To his horror, Micah at last realised that he was being given to the men at the front table for ten minutes. A lot can happen in ten minutes, he thought. Panic beat at him, but Kee was already thrusting him towards the rowdy group. The man nearest him grabbed his arm. Another man jerked off his leather cap and pulled at his hair. His captor made him kneel on the table and pushed his forehead to touch the wood, so that his ass was high in the air. Then he began to hit Micah's buttocks with a horsehair whip shouting at him as he did so. Micah understood the word. He had heard it before.

"Dance!" the man shouted. "Make your ass dance for me!"

In spite of himself, Micah began to wriggle, trying to avoid the stinging cut of the whip against his already tender flesh, but that only made his tormentor beat him harder and faster, screaming at him to dance! Dance! He jerked convulsively, his mind empty of everything but his wish to avoid the pain. He could hear the men laughing, the clink of the bottles, the belches.

Then they pulled him by the hair until he was upright, his knees splayed wide, his cock arching towards them. They began to torment his penis, flicking it lightly with the soft brush, then squeezing it with their hands, then pulling back as he threatened to find release. Their fingers pushed and poked at his balls, explored his anus. Finally, one of the men climbed up onto the table and opened his pants, pushing himself into Micah's ass. He was so drunk he came almost immediately, toppling off the table onto the ground amid the cheers of his friends. Then Micah felt the nozzle of a wine skin shoved into his anus and the wine squirted inside him. Hot tears stung his cheeks. He tried to find Attlad in the sea of faces but another man pulled him off the table so that Micah straddled him, forcing Micah to leak the mingled come and wine out of his anus onto his hairy chest. Then the rough soldier pushed the slave's face against him, making it plain that he wanted him to lick him clean. The heavy sweat, the thick come, the red sour taste of the wine threatened to gag Micah, but he forced himself to obey, sliding his tongue over the man's hairy chest slowly, swallowing the strange mingled juices.

Suddenly the time was up. Micah was pulled off his tormentor and led back to Attlad. When he stumbled, Attlad caught him in his strong arms, holding him for a long comforting moment against his muscular body. Micah squinted through his tears, unable to see clearly if his master was telling him anything. Then he felt Attlad's fingers on the palm of his hand. Micah concentrated. He placed his own hand against Attlad's bare chest.

"Again," he signed carefully.

"You did well," Attlad told him. "I am pleased. Now it is almost time for the rings."

The rings. Micah shivered. For the first time, he wondered if would survive.

FIVE

tense silence fell over the assembly as Attlad led his slave to the fire at one side of the brightly lit platform. The bottom part of the scaffold holding the chains where Micah had been hung, was shaped like a square. Micah's wrists were attached to the top corners, and his ankles at the bottom, so that his sore and aching body was stretched to form an X. Two bare chested men took up position, one behind him, one in front, and began to beat him with long pliable switches. Micah cried out and writhed, desperately trying to escape the stinging blows. The men were experienced and thorough, each blow landing in a slightly different area of his burning flesh, so that there was no part of his body that eluded the kiss of the lash, not even the insides of his thighs. When Attlad gave them the sign, they stepped back, leaving Micah gasping.

Attlad stepped close and picked up an instrument that was handed to him on a silver tray. Micah tensed again for a different kind of pain. But he was not prepared for the hot, excruciating jolt of agony that shot through his right nipple when Attlad touched it. He screamed. He struggled in earnest, twisting and pulling with all his might against the restraints. He knew it was useless, but reason had deserted him. There was nothing in his mind now but the pain and his desperate desire to avoid it. Attlad lifted his implement to the left nipple and Micah screamed again. Over and over. His raw voice rose to a piercing shriek as he felt Attlad left his stiff cock and press the instrument of torture to its root. Micah was almost mad with the pain. It took a while to realize that Attlad had stopped and was now pressing a soft cloth dipped in wine to his parched lips. He sucked at it thankfully. In the flare of the torchlight, his naked body gleamed with sweat. His face was red, slick with tears, his long hair drenched with perspiration. When Attlad reached up and pierced his right ear, Micah sobbed hopelessly. Then it was over.

Gold rings were now in his nipples. A gold chain linked them and from it dangled a gold disk with Attlad's symbol on it, as well as his name. He could feel the weight of an earring in one ear. Between his legs burned a core of pain he could not analyze.

When Attlad approached him again, Micah cried out to him, begging him for mercy, his voice a mere croak it was so hoarse from screaming. He had totally forgotten that his master could not understand his words. Attlad signalled for him to be taken down and Micah fell again into his master's arms. He clung to Attlad desperately, dimly aware that he wanted to please this man, had to please him. He knew at that moment that he would do anything Attlad commanded him, without thought or question.

Attlad's great black horse was led before them and his master vaulted easily onto its back. Micah was hoisted up in front of him and they rode out of the feast area, Attlad's strong arm around his slave who was dizzy with pain.

Attlad dismounted outside his tent and pulled Micah down into his arms. He half carried, half dragged his slave inside and threw him on the bed. Micah lay on his back, not bothering to wipe the tears from his face, and watched Attlad move about the beautiful tent, pouring wine and preparing something hot in a large basin. He came to the bed and sat down beside Micah. He began to sponge his body with clothes dipped in the steaming liquid, his hands strong, sure, possessive. When it was over, Micah rested his head on Attlad's chest and sipped wine from his master's goblet. He felt calm, now, curiously replete and accepting. He looked up into Attlad's strong face and smiled as his master stroked his hair and fondled the curls between his thighs. Micah spread his legs wider and winced as Attlad touched him there, where the fire still burned.

"Come," Attlad gestured. "Look at my love slave."

He led Micah over to a large mirror that was propped up in a corner of the tent and stood beside him, smiling. Micah stared at the exhausted image that looked back at him, the gold rings in the swollen nipples, the chain between them, the gold earring with the red teardrop suspended from it. Attlad turned him around and pushed his head down so that he could look between his legs and see his own ass. A gold ring gleamed under his cock and hanging from it was a tiny red teardrop like the one in his ear. Micah straightened up slowly and looked at Attlad.

"No one will touch you, now, without my permission," Attlad explained, moving his hands with careful precision to make sure he understood. "You are Chento, my Personal Body Slave."

Micah nodded. He understood. Attlad's mark was everywhere. Even from behind it would be obvious that he was a sex slave, the property of his master. As if reading his mind, Attlad nodded and pointed to the wine. When

Micah poured it for him, Attlad stretched out on the bed and had Micah kneel beside him, his head resting against his thigh. They stayed that way for a long time, Attlad feeding him sips of wine and talking to him in his own liquid language with its clusters of harsh consonants. Micah listened and watched, breathing in the smell of the man until gradually he began to want him. He nuzzled the man's crotch trying to get him aroused. He himself was hard and ready. He could feel Attlad's cock swelling against his eager face, but the man ignored his efforts for some time.

Finally, Attlad stood up and began to undress. Micah watched hungrily as the lean dark body emerged from the dull soldier's clothing. He lay down eagerly on his back as his master commanded. Attlad lay beside him and kissed him, toying with his tender nipples and making him wince. He made Micah straddle him, squatting over his stomach as he licked his master's salty skin, getting closer and closer to the long hard nipples that fascinated him so but that he had never been allowed to touch. Attlad lay back, his eyes soft, and let his slave cover him with wet kisses, leaving a trail of saliva on the dark skin. Then at last, Micah moved down between his legs and took his master fully into his mouth, the cock almost gagging him with its swollen size. And for the first time, his master made himself vulnerable to him, the slave, and Micah sucked him strongly, tenderly, careful to shield him from his sharp teeth. But before he had finished, Attlad pulled away and told Micah to lower himself onto his stiff member and bring him off. Micah balanced carefully over him and held the cheeks of his ass apart, opening himself to his master. Carefully, he lowered himself onto the erect cock, wincing as the painful tender skin around the ring and its jewel at the base of his own cock rubbed and stretched. The muscles in his buttocks and thighs strained as he moved himself up and down, the whole bed creaking with his exertions. Attlad arched his back. The tendons stood out on his neck as he began to moan. Micah redoubled his efforts, sweat standing out on his taut body, his own cock beginning to jerk. When Attlad came, Micah sat still, his master still inside him, not daring to move without a command. Attlad lay quietly. Then he smiled.

"Good, Chento. Lie down."

Micah obeyed. He lay still, watching Attlad sip his wine, until he was ready to take his slave again.

"Hold your ankles," Attlad ordered.

Micah lay on his back, his legs in the air as he held his ankles. Attlad pushed his legs wide apart and knelt over him, his cock swollen and hungry. He thrust deeply into Micah, making his slave catch his breath and moan as Attlad rammed himself deeper and deeper into his bowels. Micah tried not to cry out with the pain as his master banged against his sore cock, but at last it was too much and he began to whimper. Attlad exploded inside him.

For a moment, Attlad lay still, catching his breath. But he did not tell Micah to put his legs down, so the slave lay there on his back, still holding his ankles, his cock still stiff, his anus dripping with his master's come.

Then Attlad rolled him further back so the erotic eye of his ass was more accessible, and kissed the base of Micah's stiff cock. His lips were cool and soft against the burning tenderness there and Micah cried out with pleasure, his cock jerking suddenly and releasing a pearly stream of come onto the chain joining his nipples.

Attlad laughed and allowed him to put down his legs. He picked up a cool cloth and wiped off his slave and himself and lay down on the bed. Then he positioned Micah with his back to him. In a few moments, he entered his slave again, but did nothing more. He put his arms around

Micah and pulled him close.

That night, Micah fell asleep with his master's cock up his ass and dreamed of happiness.

Micah was awake instantly and completely. He did not know what had awakened him. He lay perfectly still, hearing his master's deep even breathing, the faint sound of people moving outside, the whinny of a horse. He could feel someone in the tent. From the time he was a cadet, he had been trained to react like this, taking the measure of things before leaping to attack. He ran over the layout of the tent in his mind, remembering the position of the table and chair, the bowl of spiced water on the table, the fruit, the long knife Attlad used to slice it.

Without warning, Micah leapt across the sleeping body of his master and grabbed for the knife. A young man by the opening of the tent, froze in terror, shocked that a naked slave should menace him with a weapon. Micah began to circle him, closer, closer, as the man was forced to back up, away from the one exit. The man called out in a strangled voice.

Micah felt a hand on his bare flank. His master was behind him, laughing at the frightened messenger. He was obviously pleased that Micah had leapt so unquestioningly to his defence. At once, without having to be told, Micah handed Attlad the knife, and knelt at his feet.

The messenger was now taking out his fury in harsh words, waving his arms and pointing at Micah angrily. But Attlad only smiled, one hand playing idly with Micah's long hair. As Micah watched the exchange, he realized that he had reacted purely on instinct and the training of a warrior. That part of him at least was not dead. Perhaps that should tell him something. It was time to return to being a Nebula

Warrior. He remembered his promise to Forrest and was sur-prised to find that the idea of escape, treasured for so long, brought a hint of sadness with it now.

At last the messenger seemed to realize he was wasting his energy and handed Attlad the papers he had been car-rying. Attlad glanced at them, nodded and dismissed the man.

"Chento!"

Micah's head was jerked back by the hair, punishment for not paying closer attention. Micah blinked. He watched the rapid hand signals intently, afraid of not being able to understand fast enough. It seemed his master wanted him to follow and speak to someone, or was it for someone? What could that mean?

He got to his feet and waited patiently while his mas-ter got dressed. He assumed that he, as usual, would remain naked. It was a surprise when Attlad picked up a handsome blue cloak, dropped it around his shoulders and fastened the golden clasp at his throat.

"It is cool early in the morning." Attlad smiled over his hands.

The cloak was warm against Micah's bare skin. It was long in the back, almost sweeping the ground, but shorter in front. As he walked, it swung open, revealing his nakedness underneath. He did not have to be told not to try to hold the cloak closed around him. He knew he did not have that right.

Outside, the mists were rising in the early morning coolness. The camp was already humming with activity, the fires being prepared by the house slaves in their brown uni-forms. Soldiers stood around in groups, talking together. They saluted Attlad as he passed. Micah they ignored.

Micah followed Attlad and two other soldiers along a footpath that led up the hill behind the great amphitheater.

They soon came to a clearing where a group of armed men were gathered around a kneeling figure. They parted in front of Attlad, one man speaking rapidly, obviously explaining the situation. Micah waited behind his master until he heard his name.

"Chento!"Attlad's hand made the talk sign and he pointed to the kneeling prisoner.

Micah was startled to see, when he looked at him more closely, that the man was Terran, like himself. He was filthy, his clothes ripped in many places, blood on his face and scratched arms. He had obviously been beaten. Micah felt a cold shiver of fear, in spite of the cloak. Was this a further test? Did they want to see if he would betray one his own people? Or was it simply that Nex, the translator, was sick or hungover from too much celebrating the night before? He looked into Attlad's unwavering eyes and nodded.

Attlad pointed to the ground in front of the prisoner and walked around so he was standing behind him. From here, he could watch Micah and read his signals easily.

Micah took a deep breath. He willed himself to slide to his knees, knowing the cloak would open and expose him completely to the mocking, unconquered eyes of this captured soldier. He had no choice. In one swift gesture of defiance, he unclasped the cloak and let it fall to the ground around him. The sun glinted on the golden rings on his still swollen nipples, and on the chain connecting them. It shone on the disk that bore his number and his master's symbol. He lifted his chin and threw his long hair over his shoulder.

"What is your name?" he said, his voice deep and strong in the clearing.

"So, it talks, does it?" the man drawled. Contempt was in every line of his haggard face.

"I am Chento," Micah went on. "What is your name?"

"Captain Boris Onkovsky. You must be Terran under all that hair and jewelry. Are you a prisoner, too?"

Micah paused. "I am a slave," he said simply. He might as well tell the truth. "I belong to the leader, Attlad, who is standing behind you."

"You're one of those sex slaves!" the man exclaimed, grinning. "I've heard of this but I've never seen one before. Do you like it?"

"It is my life. What were you doing when you were captured?"

"You didn't answer my question. Why should I answer yours?" He grinned. "Why are your hands always moving like that? Are you telling them what we say?"

"Yes."

"So, you are a traitor, as well as a whore!"

"I have no choice."

"There is always a choice!"

Micah shifted uneasily, his hands hesitating in their efforts to distill this conversation into his small vocabulary. He glanced at his master. Attlad was watching him intently, his grey eyes cold and dangerous.

"How were you captured?" Micah asked.

"I was patrolling sector B in my sniper, when I lost my way. I tried to explain, but they wouldn't listen."

"Perhaps they didn't understand," Micah said. He was struggling to translate 'patrol' and finally decided 'duty' would do. "What is your area of expertise?"

"I am a recon pilot. While on patrol, I'm supposed to report anything I see that's out of the ordinary. That's about it."

"And did you spot anything out of the ordinary this morning?"

"I didn't have a chance. My instruments gave out on

me and I got hopelessly off course. I made an emergency landing to try to get my bearings, but before I could contact Base Camp, I was captured by these... savages." He glared at the soldiers guarding him.

Attlad clapped his hands and Micah looked up at him at once.

"I don't believe this," muttered the captive. "Pavlov's whore."

Micah flushed, his eyes following Attlad's words, as his master walked over to join him. Naked in the sunshine, Micah got to his feet, picked up the cloak and stood beside his master. He felt very odd, looking down at the Terran soldier. Am I traitor? he wondered. Attlad finished speaking to his lieutenant and reached over to pull on Micah's chain. The unexpected pain tore through his swollen nipples, making him almost cry out. He bit down hard on his tongue. He knew the prisoner was watching and felt the hot blush of shame as his master's hand slid casually between his legs to fondle him. No! he wanted to say. Not in front of this man! But Attlad knew what he was thinking, knew the despair that went through him as Micah began to harden in spite of everything. Micah saw the knowledge in his master's grey eyes and he looked away. Attlad gave his balls a parting squeeze and withdrew his hand.

Micah was furious that this beaten Terran could make him feel such shame. I cannot stand this much longer, he thought. And he remembered Forrest and their pact. At that moment, that afternoon seemed a long way away, and he began to long for the freedom that would release him from the complex confusion of shame and desire forced on him by this situation.

Forrest had been understandably vague about the time of their meeting. It was assumed that each of them would grab the first opportunity and then wait for the other. But as the day wore on, Micah began to worry that it might not be easy to get to the river after all. Attlad kept him constantly at his side. They even rode together before lunch, Attlad urging his slave to race him the length of the field, and not satisfied with that, to jump over a series of obstacles set up in the clearing beyond. Micah was terrified of jumping, but discovered if he trusted the horse, things went fairly well. In the end, Attlad pulled him off the horse and kissed him hard on the mouth.

"Chento, we will make a rider of you yet!" he said, laughing, his hands tracing the words on Micah's bare chest under the chain.

Then he took him to the feasting place where Micah knelt at his master's side and licked up his food from a dish set on the ground. He knew when he bent over to eat, his buttocks separated to show the jewel hanging between his legs, but he was hungry, and the dream of freedom coming closer and closer made him no longer care. Attlad gave him all the wine he could drink and more, spilling it over his chest and rubbing it into his sore nipples as if it were balm.

Sitting beside them at the circular table was one of the leaders from the Hills, named Sar. Between his legs squatted his young slave. The boy was beautiful, with delicate features and long expressive hands. His shoulder- length brown hair curled against his wide cheekbones and over the silver band painted high on his forehead. His enormous dark eyes filled with devotion every time he looked at his master's face. Micah was fascinated to watch the two men, how the master always touched the slave, how their fingers twined and spoke to each other in signs no one else could see. The young slave's smooth chest glistened with oil. His hard, dark brown nipples were pierced by large gold rings, joined by a chain that looked far heavier than Micah's. The boy felt his eyes on him and looked across at Micah and smiled, laying his head against his master's knee. Sar glanced down at the boy and caressed his cheek. The expression in his face was one Micah had never seen before. There was love, and something else. Pride, he decided. Pride of ownership, of training, of being the cause of such obvious and complete devotion. Micah turned away.

But at last Attlad tired of having his slave beside him and turned to business. He dismissed Micah with a few hand signals.

"Amuse yourself for the rest of the day. I will be busy. When night comes, wait for me at the foot of my bed."

"Yes, master." He bent low and kissed Attlad's foot. As he stood up to leave, he noticed Sar's slave bent submissively over one knee as Sar used his back as a surface to write on. From what little Micah could gather, they were beginning to discuss the result of the soothsayer's vision and what it might mean for the future. Forrest had been right, after all. He would not be missed for quite a while.

With a sigh of relief, Micah fastened his cloak over his shoulders. Slowly, he walked away. Through the trees, he could see the river glinting, beckoning to him, singing its siren song of freedom.

SIX

icah was relieved that he had been allowed to keep the cloak with him since the morning. It would be good to have something to wrap himself in at night as he and Forrest made their way back to the Base. For awhile, he had been afraid that Attlad would take it from him, but the master seemed to enjoy the sight of his slave riding, with the cloak streaming out behind. It only emphasized the smooth shaven nakedness of the strong body underneath.

No one challenged Micah as he walked through the drowsy camp. He went slowly, sauntering along as if merely filling in time. There were few people about and they barely glanced at him. Once he was on the path to the river, he was alone.

When he reached the waterfall, he saw no one. Perhaps Forrest had not been able to get away after all, he thought. He took off his cloak and sat down on a smooth rock to wait. The cool hardness under his ass made him very aware of that tender part of him pierced with Attlad's mark. To his dismay, there was something erotic about the feeling and he stood up quickly and waded into the river. Even here he could not escape the ghost of Attlad's touch. It was in the water, slipping against the soft secret parts of his body that had never been exposed until he was shaved for Attlad's pleasure. He threw himself face down and began to swim fast and strong out towards the other side, trying to rid himself of the unwanted sexual energy. When he reached the opposite shore, he turned around without stopping and swam back. He emerged from the water out of breath and paused to throw his long hair off his face.

"That was quite a performance," Forrest remarked.

Micah began drying himself with the cloak. "When did you get here?"

"I was here when you arrived." Forrest eyed him speculatively.

It occurred to Micah for the first time that Forrest didn't like him very much. Micah wrapped himself in the cloak and began to braid his hair the way he used to back at the Base.

"Are you sure you want to do this?" Forrest said.

"I'm here, aren't I?"

"Frankly, that surprises me," Forrest said coolly. "I brought some clothes for you." He dropped a bundle of brown clothing similar to what he wore himself beside Micah.

Without a word, Micah stood up and put on the uniform. It felt odd. The rough material of the tunic rubbed his tender nipples, making them hard. The pants were tight, obviously meant for a smaller man. For the first time in months, Micah touched his cock and sensitive balls, trying to arrange everything into a more comfortable position. The long forbidden act made him feel guilty. Forrest watched, a sly smile on his narrow face.

Micah turned on him. "You need me, Forrest!" he

exclaimed angrily. "Remember that."

"You don't have to remind me." Forrest looked back at him, the smile gone from his face. "Look, I'm sorry. Let's start again, okay? Let bygones be bygones?" He held out his hand.

Micah shook the proferred hand readily, but he wasn't at ease with Forrest any more. He sensed a great anger at him that he didn't understand, but he could think of no way to approach it. Perhaps it was just nerves, he thought. Forrest had been a slave for a long time. He must be unsure just what he was running back to. The thought gave Micah pause. Did he know himself what he was going back to? Royal was dead. He had no family here. He hadn't been at the Base long enough to make many friends.

"Let's go," Forrest said, shouldering his small pack. "I've made a sort of raft down below the water fall. That should get us far enough downstream to throw them off the scent. When it's night, you can take over."

"Fine with me."

Micah followed Forrest along the path for some time to where it turned back towards higher ground. Forrest scrambled down the steep bank with Micah right behind him. They were below the water fall here and the roar of the cataract was like thunder. The two men climbed over boulders and fallen trees along the shore line, until the water became more calm and they could hear each other's voices above the noise of the fast flowing river. Around the next bend in the stream, Forrest stopped.

"It isn't much," he said, pointing to where several small tree trunks had been lashed together to form a rough raft.

"How do you steer it?" Micah asked.

"You don't."

Micah shrugged and inspected the knots holding the craft together. They were tight and professional, every bit as good as he could have done himself. He wondered where Forrest had learned this skill.

"I figured we could push it into the middle with poles," Forrest went on, watching him. "The current's pretty fast for awhile. It should work, don't you think?"   For the first time, he appealed directly to Micah, his voice turning anxious.

"It'll work," Micah said shortly. He picked up one of the long poles lying beside the raft and hefted it in his hands. "Let's do it."

At once, as if he had been waiting for a signal, Forrest threw his pack on board and together they waded into the cold water, pushing the raft in front of them. When the craft was free of the rocks, they climbed on board and began to pole their way into the center of the river.

The raft was heavy and awkward. In spite of everything they did, it began to turn slowly, picking up speed as the current caught it. Their poles were soon useless to them and when Forrest tried to slow them down with his, the current snatched it out of his hands. If it hadn't have been for Micah's strong arm, he would have been dragged after it into the frothing water.

With a shout of warning, Micah pulled him down beside him onto the rough logs. They were moving fast, now, the shoreline only a blur of green and grey. The raft tilted and rolled as it was swept along, the two passengers clinging to the few sawed off branches that stuck up here and there on their craft. Forrest's light brown hair was plastered to his head, his knuckles white with tension. Micah was wet through, too. Although he realized the current would slow eventually, he hoped it happened before they were upended by rocks.

At last the river opened into a wide channel and the water began to smooth out. Forrest breathed an audible sigh of relief and sat back on his heels to look about him.

"I wonder how far we've come?" he said. "Any idea?"

Micah tried to calculate the distance judging by speed and time, but a raft on a river wasn't his usual element, and he knew any calculation he would make would be far off the mark.

"I couldn't even guess," he said at last.

The remark seemed to irritate Forrest, who turned his back and watched the scenery go by in silence.

"I can't make computations without my instruments," Micah explained mildly. Forrest didn't answer.

They floated downstream for a long time, until at last Micah suggested they take their craft to shore and have something to eat. It proved much harder than they expected. The rough boat was very difficult to manoeuver, and at last, they both jumped out and began to push it in to shore. But the current was still too strong and the raft got away from them, plunging on its way down the middle of the river.

Forrest started after it, but in a few moments, he saw how impossible it was and turned, trying to make for shore. The water pushed against him, tugging and turning, washing into his mouth so that he gulped and sputtered for air. Desperately he struggled, his head disappearing and reappearing in the fast- flowing water.

Micah could see he was making no headway, and swam to him at once. Holding him with one arm, he stroked back to the shore and dragged Forrest up on dry land.

"Just when our clothes were beginning to dry," Micah remarked. He took off his tunic and pants and laid them out on a rock in the sun. Forrest sat up, coughed and caught his breath.

"You saved my life," he said.

"You'd better get out of those wet clothes so they'll

have a chance to dry. It gets quite cold out here at night, I imagine."

After a moment's hesitation, Forrest took off his clothes and laid them beside Micah's. Then he stretched out on his back and watched the water, his face tense.

"It doesn't matter about the raft," Micah said. "If my memory of the stars serves me, we have to turn north now anyway, so we couldn't have used it much longer." He lay down beside Forrest on his stomach. The sun was warm and caressing on his back. The rushing power of the river, which had been such a threat a few moments ago, was now a soothing backdrop to the warm afternoon.

After a few moments, he raised his head to look at Forrest. "Do you want —" He stared in shock. Forrest was bending over, picking up his tunic. Before he could straighten up, Micah caught sight of a raw red gash between his legs where his balls should be.

Forrest turned his head and met Micah's shocked gaze, his eyes hard and angry. "Now you know," he said. He began to dry his hairy chest with his tunic. Micah looked away in confusion. "Not a pretty sight, is it?" Forrest went on. "I don't imagine it'll be a pretty sight to my wife, either, but what can you do?"

"Forrest, I'm sorry."

"You should be!"

"What!"

"Look, Chento, I don't want to talk about this, okay?" Forrest began to put on the damp pants with jerky movements.

Micah turned away and wrapped himself in his cloak. He was shaking. It wasn't the cold, but the deep, hurting anger in Forrest's voice, in his face when he looked at him. Micah was afraid to ask why. He was afraid he knew the answer. He got to his feet without another word, walked a little way down the river and sat down an a soft tuft of grass out of sight of his companion. In the murmuring silence, he gazed out over the churning expanse of the river. He would have to say something to Forrest. But what? How can you talk about something as brutal and devastating as castration? Compared to that, everything that had happened to him was merely superficial.

By the time Micah came back and got into his dry clothes, Forrest had opened his pack and produced powered protein which he had mixed with water to make the familiar-tasting drink. He handed a bottle of it to Micah without a word.

"Thanks." Micah sat down opposite him and began to drink. "When did they do that to you?" he said at last. He had to know.

"The night I fell for your golden tresses in the traitorous moonlight," Forrest said. Micah winced. "Look, it wasn't your fault, okay? I know that. At least, my mind knows that. But I can't help being bitter."

"I understand," Micah whispered.

"No you don't. You're not the one going back to your wife only half a man!"

"At least you have someone to go back to!" cried Micah. "My lover is dead!" Micah knew that wasn't the point, but he couldn't help being defensive.

"You can find someone else! You people always do!"

"What the fuck is that supposed to mean?"

"Just what I said! You can find someone else. There's no magic cure for me!"

"You dismiss my loss just like that?"

"Look, let's just forget it, okay? I'm not thinking too straight. I know what I feel is illogical, but I can't help it."

"Anger is an emotion," Micah pointed out. "Of course it's not logical."

"Fine. Let's leave it at that." Forrest began to put his kit back together again.

It was getting dark. Around them, the shadows began to lengthen and the wind picked up.

"We should get back from the river," Micah suggested. "The water level might rise at night, if it gets windy."

"There's a cave back here," Forrest said. "I took a walk while you were away and found it. Come on. I'll show you."

Micah followed him up the bank to a small cave in the rocks above them. Together they cleared the rocks and branches from the floor and gathered moss and soft leaves which they spread for a mattress. Then they settled down for the night, each on his own side of the small space.

The wind rose. The air grew chill. The river ran swiftly down below in the cold moonlight. Micah shivered, even though he was wrapped in his warm cloak. He knew he was stronger, better able to cope with physical discomfort than his companion.

"Forrest, this is ridiculous," he said at last. He took off the cloak and threw it towards his companion.

"Shit!" said Forrest.

Muffled sounds. Then silence.

"Shit!" said Forrest again. "Chento, get your ass over here! It's freezing."

Micah bristled. He knew Forrest was goading him, using his slave name. Giving him orders. But Micah's heavy guilt made him wonder for a moment if he should swallow his pride and obey. Perhaps it would make things easier to bear for Forrest. But he couldn't bring himself to do it. He stood up abruptly. He went to the mouth of the cave, leaned against the rock and looked up at the stars. He heard Forrest moving about behind him but he didn't turn around.

"What do the stars say?" Forrest asked at last. He dropped part of the cloak over Micah's shoulders. "Do they say how to get home?"

"If you know how to read them. See that bright ring of stars straight ahead through the branches of that tree? To the right is the sword of Orion. Imagine a line from the hilt down through the tip, pointing at the ground. That's Base Station 1."

"How do you know?"

"It's part of my training." He pointed to another group of stars and explained how they showed the location of the Complex. "When they tied me up outside on the terrace at night, I used to sit and study the sky, trying to read the map spread out for me up there. There is great power in the stars. Some people can read their futures that way. I never was very good at that part."

"Maybe it's just as well." Forrest yawned. "Let's go to sleep."

They lay down side by side this time with the cloak covering them both, careful to keep a few inches of space between them. As he drifted off to sleep, Micah felt Forrest's warm breath on the back of his neck.

Micah dreamed about Attlad. They were riding together on the same horse, with Micah in front. Attlad's warm hand lay on his slave's genitals. Micah moaned and reached behind him to pull his body closer to his master. A rough punch on the shoulder woke him. Forrest was shaking him angrily.

"Get your hands off me!" Forrest demanded.

"I was dreaming, okay?"

"You want to know if I'm still capable of fucking you, is that it?" cried Forrest, pounding at Micah in a frenzy of blows. "You want to satisfy your curiosity?"

Micah pulled away and caught his wrists, forcing his hands to his sides. He was stronger and much more knowledgeable about fighting than Forrest. And he was not filled with anger. As he held the other man immobile, he felt Forrest's body begin to shake. Instinctively he pulled the man into his arms. Forrest shuddered against him and at last, his body convulsed into sobs. Micah just held him, careful not to caress him in any way, until the storm had passed. Forrest drew away.

"I really was dreaming," Micah said gently.

Forrest wiped his face on his sleeve. "I don't mean to blame you. It's just that you bring out all the bitterness. And you make me realize how much they've changed me."

"I know what you mean."

"No, you don't! I was never like this before! I was never attracted to another man in my life! But you? You have only become what you were potentially before you came here."

"What do you mean?"

"The first time I looked at you in the daylight, I saw your lover's initials burned into your ass."

"But I wanted Royal to do that."

"Exactly, just like you want to go back to Attlad, now."

"No!"

"You wear his mark between your legs. You haven't even tried to get rid of his symbol on your chest! You see, I know you, Chento! I watched how you were with that man! Do you think I'm blind and dumb?"

"You don't know what you're talking about," said Micah wearily.

"Look, I made a choice to escape. I want you to feel free to make a choice, too."

"I did!"

"Did you? Answer me one thing. What were you dreaming about just now?"

"I don't remember."

Forrest laughed. "Liar," he whispered. He reached out

and ran his fingers over Micah's cheek and into his hair. Without warning, he drew back his hand and slapped Micah across the face. "That's what you want, isn't it?" He slapped him again. "Is that what you were dreaming about?"

Micah knocked Forrest to the ground with one blow. "Shut up!"

Forrest didn't move. He made no sound. Uneasy, Micah reached down to him, feeling for his face in the darkness. "Are you okay?"

Forrest caught his hand and held it. "You pack quite a wallop," he said. His voice was casual but his hands were caressing.

Micah allowed himself to be pulled down on the ground beside Forrest. He raised his hips while Forrest pulled down his pants with quick jerks. He was breathing hard. Micah tried to kiss him but Forrest pushed him away, and knelt between his legs. Forrest's eager hands paused on Micah's balls, touching the ring with its jewel.

"Shit," he muttered softly. "It makes me feel like Attlad's watching us."

"There's no one here," Micah said, raising his legs.

Forrest pushed into him and pumped fiercely, grunting with effort. He came in a rising crescendo and fell over Micah, panting.

In a minute, he rolled over on his back and pulled Micah on top of him. "Your turn," he said briefly.

Micah was already erect. He rubbed his cock in Forrest's come and gently spread Forrest's legs. He lifted the man's hips and ran one hand down between his crack. Feeling the scared, stretched tissue behind the base of his penis, Micah hesitated.

"Go on," hissed Forrest between his teeth.

Micah slipped the tip of his penis inside Forrest and waited for the other man to relax. Then he held on to his hips and slowly pushed deeper inside. Forrest caught his breath. When he began to thrust up with his hips, Micah started to move in and out, deeper, deeper. He became caught up in his own rhythm, working faster and faster until he came.

"Now we can both get some sleep," Forrest said, pulling up his pants.

They lay down again, side by side. Micah considered several things he might say to his friend, but dismissed them all. He understood the gesture as one of forgiveness. Trying to put it into words would only embarrass his friend.

When Micah woke up next, Forrest was no longer beside him. Micah raised his head, listening. Outside he thought he heard a faint rustling of leaves. Forrest was probably taking a leak, he thought. Micah turned over and went back to sleep.

Next time he awoke, it was dawn. Forrest was gone again. Micah got up and went to the mouth of the cave, but there was no sign of his companion. Uneasy, Micah made his way down to the river. Spread out on a rock were three packets of protein, a plastic bottle to mix them in and a peach. A note was scratched in the sand.

'Thanks. Now I know my way. It's up to you to find yours.'

SEVEN

icah walked. Hour after hour, in daylight and darkness and the twilight time in between, he walked. And always he headed towards the star formation he had spent so much time studying while he was tied up on the terrace in the early evening.

He was going back to Attlad. He knew he would be punished, and the fear twisted inside his stomach and made his heart beat faster. But the real dread was that Attlad might reject him. When this thought came, his body went cold and his mind closed off defensively. If this happened, his life was over. Perhaps in the end, his suffering, his rejection of his own people, all would be for nothing. But he refused to consider this for long. He kept his mind focused on his total submission to his master. He would give as he had never given before and in the end, he would merge with Attlad and they would both be stronger. In this was his power, his strength and his whole purpose in living.

When had he come to realize what Attlad meant to him? When had it finally occurred to him that all his life he had been searching for the perfect master and that with Attlad, he was at last living his secret fantasy? It had taken Forrest's sharp words to bring it all into focus. He had fought the knowledge automatically because he had been trained to fight anyone who might capture him, to view this person as 'the enemy'. Even the hint of fraternization would be viewed as a breach of trust. As a full fledged Nebula Warrior, it would have been traitorous for him to consider his new life as acceptable in any way.

After a while, his fatigue, his bruised and aching feet, and the hunger that began to gnaw at him continually kept his mind occupied. He knew he would accept whatever punishment was given him. He would suffer it all for Attlad. It took far longer getting back to the Complex, since he had no swift running river to help him. Now it was all uphill and he often had to go far out of his way because of the cliffs and huge slate-smooth rocks that towered high above the river. But he kept on going.

At last he began to recognize landmarks. And he began to have the strong feeling that he was being watched. He knew there were lookouts posted for miles around the Complex, but he never saw anyone. He was not challenged. Far from reassuring him, this filled him with sick apprehension, but he kept on going, until one day, around noon, he climbed the steps to the main gate and walked past the sentries into the courtyard.

There were soldiers standing about and guards and men with horses. And they all looked at him curiously. But still no one stopped him or interfered with him in any way. Micah knew Attlad often spent these hours going over reports on his private terrace above the second courtyard, and he went through the final gate into the inner yard. Here he stopped and looked up. His master sat at a table conferring with three of his men. A long narrow flight of stairs led up to the terrace with two armed men guarding the foot.

Micah stepped into the middle of the courtyard and took out his braid so that his long blond hair blew free in the breeze. Next, he pulled off his tunic and stepped out of his pants so that he at last stood naked in the sunshine in the court below where his master sat. Attlad watched without expression as Micah walked over to the steps and went down on his knees. Slowly and painfully he climbed up the steps this way, his hands locked behind him. It took quite a while but at last he knelt at the top and bowed his head before Attlad.

There was no sound from any of the men. No word and no gesture. Then he felt a booted foot on his shoulder and he was shoved hard. He fell backwards, rolling helplessly down the stairs until he lay bruised and bleeding at the foot. After a moment, he looked up. Attlad had returned to talking and was paying no attention to him. Gritting his teeth, Micah started up the steps, again on his knees. It was much more painful now, but he went on until once again he knelt at the top. This time a leather whip whistled across his bare shoulders. Once. Twice. The third time he lost his balance and fell, but he had the presence of mind to shield his head. He sprawled on the stones at the bottom, his head buzzing, his shoulder throbbing with pain. He was too stunned to try again. He stayed where he was, unmoving at the foot of the stairs, the sun beating down on his back, the flies settling on his bleeding scrapes and gashes. He could only hope that Attlad might at last take pity on him and relent.

Finally, Micah realized he must have passed out. He felt a rough hand pulling at his hair and he struggled up on all fours. He didn't dare look up to see who was dragging him along. He knew it wasn't Attlad by the voice and the way the man walked. It was late, now. He had no idea how long he had lain in the courtyard. He was light-headed from hunger and dizzy from the sun. His mouth was dry, and he found it hard to move quickly. Cool polished stone floors under his knees and hands told him they were now inside, but it took all his strength to keep moving. He had no idea where he was until a jerk on his hair pulled him into an upright position, still on his knees, and he saw they were in the grooming room.

Kee was looking down at him, a whip in his hand. Micah blinked against the bright lights of the room and wondered if he would have the strength to take a beating now. But Kee put down the whip and pointed to the table. Micah pulled himself unsteadily to his feet. He would have fallen if Simon hadn't appeared and helped him up on the table. The big man gave his arm a special squeeze as he looked down at him. Micah thanked him with his eyes.

Kee was preparing a needle which he then jabbed roughly into Micah's thigh. All the time he was grumbling to Simon. He seemed angry. He pushed Micah's legs apart and fingered the red tear drop, pinching Micah's balls painfully as he did so. Then he prepared his shaving things and proceeded to shave Micah all over. Micah was used to the procedure by now, but it still made him tense. Especially since he sensed such hostility from Kee and realized he would probably relish a slip of the hand, if he thought he could get away with it.

When Kee had finished, Simon sponged off Micah's body and rubbed soothing oil into his skin. His strong hands seemed to be checking for breaks and sprains, moving his wrists and ankles and knees, making sure everything was still in working order after his falls down the stairs. Then he had Micah kneel on the table and fed him from the silver bottle. When that was over, Micah felt a little better. They left him alone for a few moments. But soon they were back.

"Bend over." Kee's hand signals were sharp and angry,

like his voice. When Micah obeyed, Kee shoved a long smooth pellet up his anus, then ordered him to sit on the table, while he tidied up the room. Micah swayed with fatigue as the watched the man put away the oils and razors and soap. Kee caught his arm, pulled him off the table and made him squat on the floor over a large bowl. In a few minutes, his bowels emptied with a rush and the smell of his excrement filled the room. Micah's face flushed a deep red as Kee upended him over his knee and thrust the bulb of the enema into him, filling his insides with warm water, washing out more filth. When this was over, Kee wiped Micah's ass and pushed him down on all fours again. Simon clipped a thin lead to the chain between his nipples and gave it a gentle tug. Micah winced. He bit his lip hard and began to follow Simon, trying hard to keep up so the leash wouldn't pull again on the sensitive nipples.

They went down corridors and through doors. They passed many house slaves, judging by the bare feet, and several booted soldiers. At last they stopped. Micah looked up to find himself outside Attlad's door. His stomach constricted with fear. Simon was carrying something in his other hand which he now placed on the floor to one side of the door. It was a rod with clamps on each end. He explained with his hands that Micah was to place a knee in each clamp, so that the contraption made it impossible to bring his legs together. When he complied, Simon locked them that way and told him to put his head on the ground. His hands were locked behind his back. Simon hung one end of the leash over a hook in the wall and left him.

Micah had never experienced such shame. He felt like an animal, casually tied up outside his master's door. No explanation. No words to calm the fear, the terrible anxiety that he might be forgotten. Or worse. His forehead, forced against the floor, throbbed with the unaccustomed task of supporting so much of his weight. His thighs were forced so far apart that the muscles screamed. The globes of his ass were thrust high in the air by this degrading position, an enticing target for every passer by. The first time he heard footsteps approaching along the corridor and saw the boots stop beside him, Micah cringed. But he didn't dare look up to see who it was and the man only laughed and passed on, trailing his fingernail along the crack in Micah's buttocks before he left.

After a while, he lost track of the numbers of men who passed by, the rough touches he had to endure, although he knew none of them would dare to really hurt him. He was Attlad's property, even if he was being punished. Finally, it must have been hours later, someone stopped and opened the door. The boots looked familiar.

"Attlad!" Micah struggled to raise his head, but he was so stiff and sore that it was difficult to get his balance and Attlad was gone by the time he had manoeuvered himself into a more upright position. The only one he could see was Kee, grinning down at him. He had a particularly unpleasant expression in his eyes, a mingling of contempt and something else. Triumph? Kee reached over and gave the leash a series of rough jerks that brought a cry of pain from Micah as his nipples were pulled unmercifully. Then Kee laughed and opened Attlad's door and went inside.

Micah was stunned. What did that mean? Kee wasn't an officer. He wouldn't have messages to deliver or business to discuss with Attlad. When Micah finally faced the truth, he laid his head down on the floor and moaned in pain. He thought he couldn't stand the knowledge that Kee was with his master. The picture in his mind of Kee naked in his master's bed burned into Micah's mind giving him such intense agony that he writhed on the ground, pulling the leash and hurting his own nipples.

"It's my own fault!" he told himself tearfully. "I should never have left him! I deserve to be punished, but please! Please not this way!" At last, exhausted with his own grief and pain, he fell asleep, on his knees on the stone floor outside his master's bedroom.

Micah was tied up and exposed outside Attlad's door for three days and nights. Twice a day Simon would come and feed him from the bottle. He would reach over and take Micah's limp cock and put it into the plastic bottle so he could relieve himself. Once in the morning he would take him to the grooming room to have a suppository thrust up his ass so he could void himself over the basin. Then Simon or Kee would take him over their knee and give him an enema, and wipe his ass clean again. Then back to his post outside Attlad's door. And every night Kee would arrive, his face gleaming with satisfaction. And he always pulled viciously at Micah's leash, causing great agony to his abused nipples. Micah lay on the floor, filled with despair, and a numb acceptance.

The fourth day, when Simon brought him back from the grooming room, he didn't lock his knees into the clamps. Micah assumed the position anyway and Simon patted his cheek before he left. Late that night, Kee opened the door and unclipped Micah's chain.

"Attlad wants you in here," he said, his face blank, his hands barely moving enough to complete the words. He was wearing nothing but a leather jock strap.

Micah fell when he tried to move. He picked himself up and shuffled stiffly forward on all fours. Attlad was seated in his armchair beside the bed, wearing a robe. At once Micah touched his forehead to the floor and sat up on his haunches waiting for some signal.

"Kee wants entertainment." Attlad's gestures were lazy. He took a sip of wine and stared down at Micah, his eyes hard, unreadable.

Micah began to sweat. "Whatever pleases you, master," he said, his hands shaking. He was deathly afraid. Whatever Attlad wanted he must do, willingly and well. His master had to take him back!

"Come here."

Micah scurried across the room and knelt before him. Attlad picked up a brass bell about the size of a large nut and attached it to the ring in Micah's left nipple. Micah caught his breath. The bell was surprisingly heavy. He gritted his teeth as Attlad hooked a similar bell to the other nipple and signalled him to crawl around the room.

Micah obeyed at once. The bells tinkled dully as he moved, and every sound meant a pull at his nipples. When he arrived back before Attlad, his master studied him consideringly.

Then he took a short roll of leather and forced it between Micah's teeth. On each end were brass rings. Attlad clipped a leather lead onto Micah's right nipple ring beside the bell, threaded it through the brass circles of the gag and attached the other end to the other nipple. Then Attlad reached over and picked up his whip. But instead of hitting his slave, as Micah expected, Attlad shoved the handle up his ass, so that the leather thongs hung down to the floor, like a tail.

"Now Kee will put you through your paces." Attlad smiled, a cruel, cold smile that made Micah break out in a sweat. "Ride him, Kee." The meaning of the words was obvious.

Kee laughed and straddled Micah, jouncing up and down on his back. Then Micah felt the sharp smack of a riding crop against his flanks and he began to lurch around the room again as fast as he could, considering his stiff joints. He found it hard to concentrate, to remember to clench the handle in his ass. Trying to breathe with the gag in his mouth was also difficult, and all the time Kee's heavy body swayed on top of him. But he couldn't move fast enough to please his rider and the crop descended in a fast tatoo on his bare flanks. The bells tormented his nipples more and more, the faster he went, as he jerked and stumbled ahead. And every time they came to the end of the room, Kee pulled viciously on the bridle, tearing at first one nipple, then the other. Micah arrived back in front of Attlad covered in sweat, his face red and bloated with tears. But still Attlad wasn't satisfied.

"You will do it faster this time. I am timing you."

Around they went again, Micah and his tormentor. The only thought in his head now was getting back to Attlad and stopping the constant blows, the stinging pain, the hurting jerking pull at his nipples. But this time he was not allowed to stop. Around and around the room they went until Micah lost all sense of what of he was doing and began to try to get rid of Kee, bucking and feinting in an effort to unseat him. The dull tinkle of the bells became confused in his mind with the suffering they caused him, so that he began to think the hated sound was causing him the agony. If only he could escape from the sound, the torture would stop.

At last, Attlad called a halt to the sport and allowed Micah to lie at his feet for a moment, panting as he tried to get his breath. Still he remembered to keep his sphincter muscles clenched so that the whip wouldn't slip out. His body was streaked with sweat, now, his ass striped with red welts from the whip. He felt as if his buttocks were swollen to twice their size, but all he cared about was that Attlad would be satisfied. When he looked up at that dark face, he couldn't tell.

Hesitantly, Micah raised his hands to sign his plea.

"Forgive me," he said.

"Why?"

"I will do anything to please you," Micah sobbed.

"Of course. You are a slave." Attlad shrugged.

"I am yours." Micah wished his head were a bit clearer. He couldn't seem to collect his thoughts enough to present a proper argument.

"You still have to satisfy Kee," Attlad said. "You are his for the next few minutes." Attlad sat back, drinking wine as, with a heavy heart, Micah crawled over to Kee.

The man looked at Micah with contempt as he yanked the whip out of his ass. Then he reached down and took a handful of Micah's damp hair and pulled him to his feet. With a snarl of utter hatred, he threw Micah over the bar at the end of the bed. Micah thought his back might break and reached out blindly for support. Kee knocked his hands away. Then, very deliberately, Kee raped him. He was rough, vicious, his thrusts crushing Micah's balls each time. Micah turned his head and looked at Attlad through his tears, but his master's face was without expression. Just before he came, Kee reached down and pulled on the bells, making Micah scream.

When it was over, Micah didn't think he could move on his own, but Kee dragged him onto his knees before Attlad where he crouched, trembling with shock and pain and exhaustion, feeling his enemy's warm juices drip down his legs. He could see his master was aroused and for a wild moment, he thought Attlad was going to dismiss Kee and take his slave to bed.

Instead, he was told to kneel and watch as Attlad motioned Kee onto the bed and thrust his swollen cock up the man's hated ass. But Micah watched, because he had been ordered to, though every thrust caused him much more pain than he had experienced up till now. His own penis was soon stiff, arcing towards the couple on the bed with its own aching desire. Micah cried quietly as Attlad and Kee both came.

At last, Attlad dismissed his servant, and for a while, nothing happened. But Micah's pain and humiliation were not over for that night. Suddenly, Attlad pulled his slave by his hair up and over his knee and began to hit him with his bare hand. The strong, sharp blows shook Micah to the depths of his being, going through his buttocks first, then penetrating to his soul. There was something so very personal about it that for the first time Micah realized the depth of the man's passionate anger against him. He could feel the tensing of Attlad's body as he swung back his arm and brought it down again. He cried out, again and again, begging forgiveness for his desertion. The muscles of his ass danced under his master's hand.

When it was over, Attlad pushed him off and he fell to the floor. He was breathing hard. "Surely he'll be satisfied now," Micah thought, struggling to his knees. He could barely see his master through his tears.

Attlad took a series of steel clips from a drawer. He made Micah lean back, supporting himself on his hands behind him on the floor, so that he was exposed and powerless before his master. Attlad fastened a leather gag in his mouth and covered his eyes with a leather blindfold. Micah was truly terrified, now. His whole body was shaking. He felt Attlad remove the bells from his rings. But before he could savor any relief, a sudden hot pain shot through his right nipple as Attlad attached one of the clamps. Micah struggled against the gag, fighting with his own self-control to keep from pushing himself away from the pain Attlad was inflicting on him. He wore no restraints. A real test. Attlad took Micah's stiff cock in one hand and attached a clamp to each side and at the base. He put another two on each ball.

Behind the gag, Micah was screaming.

Not being able to see the man, meant he couldn't tell where the attack would come from next, couldn't prepare or control the gasps that made his chest heave. But through the pain, he could hear Attlad's voice, and although he couldn't understand the words, he was glad of that thin thread of communication between them. Occasionally he heard his own name; Chento.   Just when he thought things couldn't get worse, Attlad began to take off the clamps and this agony was even more excruciating as the blood rushed back. He almost lost his balance and Attlad dragged him upright again. Still he refused to pull his legs together, to protect himself in any way from this man who had total power over him. He would allow him any rights, any liberties. Attlad could inflict any indignity to his slave's body. And Micah would give. And give some more.

When it was over, Attlad took off the blindfold and the gag. Micah blinked. He laid his head against Attlad's bare thigh and his master stroked his hair.

"Forgive me!" Micah pleaded with shaking hands.

Attlad sat down and offered Micah a sip of his wine. "No P.B has ever run off from me," Attlad said.

"I came back."

"You think it is that easy?"

Micah went cold. "No," he said. "It is never easy."

Attlad went to the communication device by the wall and spoke into the mouthpiece. A few moments later, a man arrived at the door whom Micah did not recognize. He was carrying a box in one hand and a stool in the other. He bowed to Attlad and sat down on the stool.

Micah stood in front of him, his legs apart, as usual. The stool was high, and the man took Micah's erect cock and fitted it into a clamp attached to the stool. Micah looked at Attlad, panic in his eyes.

"You wear my rings, and my jewel," Attlad told him, "but these things can be removed. The mark which this man will put on you, cannot be removed."

"Oh God!" Micah clenched his fists as the man's needle hummed into life.

Attlad came to stand behind him, one arm around Micah's chest. Micah clutched convulsively at the hard muscled forearm as the needle cut into his penis. He buried his scream against his master's arm, but his cock remained rigid, exposing it's thick shaft to the tattoo artist's needle. Gradually, as Micah struggled to control his cries, a small red and blue dragon that was Attlad's symbol, took shape along his penis. The man worked quickly, obviously an expert in his job. When he was finished, he wiped Micah's cock with a stinging solution, put away his instruments, bowed to Attlad and left.

Micah was shaking. His cock felt swollen to twice its size as it throbbed with hot pain. He would have slipped to his knees if Attlad had not held him up and poured a little wine down his throat. Then Attlad led his slave to the foot of the bed and fastened his wrists to the top of the bed posts, and his ankles to the bottom.

All night long, Micah hung at the foot of his master's bed. At times, he drifted into a semi-conscious state and, for a while, he was not aware of his pain. Then he would open his eyes again, and the ache and anguish would return. He watched his master sleep, glad, that at least he had not been turned around the other way so that he could not see the object of his devotion. Micah knew there would be more tests before Attlad was satisfied. If only he could endure, there was hope.

EIGHT

t dawn, Attlad took Micah down from his restraints at last and held him in his arms. Micah's blue eyes filled with tears of gratitude. He opened his mouth against the man's broad chest and licked the salt from his skin. Attlad made soothing noises, one hand caressing his slave between the legs. Then his hand moved to Micah's thigh and began to make signs there. Micah stopped licking to concentrate.

"You are going away, master?"

"Wait here. Sleep at the foot of my bed. I will return."

"When?"

"Sleep, Chento. You must get back your strength for me."

"Yes, master." He fell asleep in his master's arms.

When he woke up, Attlad was gone. Micah prowled around the large room uneasily. He wished he had some idea of how long Attlad would be away. It made him feel very insecure, just being left like that. Royal was gone. Forrest had walked off. Now Attlad. Although the circumstances were quite different, the similarities made him uneasy.

He went into the luxurious bathing room and took a shower. He washed his hair, dried it, brushed it for a long time. He was hungry, but all he could find in the room was wine and some fruit. A few bottles of protein were in the cupboard. Were they meant for him? Or were they Attlad's? Would he be punished if he drank them without permission? Perhaps this, too, was a test.

At last, he opened the door, hoping to catch sight of Simon, or even Kee. On the floor was a large bowl filled with his usual breakfast of milk and broken biscuits. Micah carried the bowl out onto the private terrace and put it on the floor. He knelt in front of it and began to eat, picking up the biscuits with his teeth and lapping up the milk with his tongue. He was getting quite proficient at it by now.

After eating, he felt better. For a while, he sat in the sun, relaxing. His penis was slightly swollen, the red and blue dragon shrunken now, into a smaller, less menacing creature altogether. Micah smiled. When his master returned, the dragon would be elongated and fierce again.

After a while, Micah got bored with nothing to do. He put his bowl back outside the door and began to go through a series of exercises, pushups, balancing on his hands, swinging from the chains attached to the ceiling. He began to poke into the drawers and cupboards, looking through his master's supply of cloaks and tunics and leggings and polished high leather boots. He lingered over the boots, breathing in the rich evocative smell of the leather. He took out a sheaf of papers from a drawer and studied the symbols that covered them. They were unintelligible to him, no matter how he puzzled over them. He studied the letters on the disk on his chest. Knowing what this said and how it was pronounced, gave him something to work on, but it was not enough. After a few hours, he had made out his own name on one of the papers. The name was repeated in several places, along with a series of what he thought must be numbers.

"A bill of sale," he decided. But he determined to learn how to read this language he was beginning to decipher. He missed reading. One of the fond memories he still carried from his former life was reading out loud to Royal in the evenings. Perhaps someday he would be able to read to Attlad. Perhaps...when he learned the language.

Dinner appeared outside the door and Micah ate the rich stew out on the terrace as well. This time, there was a bottle of protein provided. He wondered if it would be all right to pick it up and drink it himself. He had never been allowed to do this before, but how else was he supposed to drink it? At last, he decided on a compromise. He opened the bottle, poured its contents into his bowl, and licked it up with his tongue. After another session of calisthenics, he lay down across the foot of the huge bed and fell asleep.

In the morning, Attlad had not returned. Micah felt bereft, as if part of him were actually missing. He went through his calisthenics, ate his breakfast on the terrace. He longed to go outside, to run in the field or even go for a ride, but none of this had been mentioned by Attlad. After a while, Micah opened a drawer at the bottom of the cupboard and studied the selection of swords he had found there the day before. He took them out, one by one, hefted them, checking the weight, the dimensions. They were heavier than what he was used to, and slightly longer, crafted for taller men to use in real battles. He selected the one closest to the model he had trained with and took it outside on the terrace. Here, he began to go through the long, slow routine he had been doing every day since he was a 15 year old cadet, learning to handle arms. Any sword, of course, was primitive to Micah, but it was perfect for learning balance, the thrust and parry of hand to hand combat, the quickness and agility useful for even the most advanced weapon. There were twelve positions, each one important, each one another stage in a slow, balanced, single movement that was simplicity itself to watch, but extremely difficult to do well. It took great concentration and control.

Micah was so completely into this exercise, that he did not hear Attlad come onto the terrace. He was not aware of him until he had finished the exercise and looked up to see his master leaning one shoulder against the door. At once he sank to his knees and offered the sword to Attlad.

Attlad shook his head and pulled Micah to his feet. "Come to the gym," he said. "Let's see how good you really are."

Micah went cold. Was this to be another test? Would he be expected to lose to his master? If he won, would he be punished? If he lost on purpose, would it be seen and would he be punished for that, too? On the other hand, Attlad was an experienced soldier. He might win easily over Micah, in spite of the Terran's training and the prizes he had won at exhibition matches.

All this was going through Micah's head as he watched Attlad change into a leather tunic and leggings. Micah was wondering if he would be expected to fight naked, which would be a great disadvantage, when Attlad handed him a leather tunic and leggings as well.

"Tie back your hair and come with me."

Micah tied his hair into a pony tail with the leather thong Attlad gave him and picked up the sword he had been working with. He followed his master to the gym.

It felt very strange walking through the corridors fully dressed for the first time. With every move, he was aware of the leather sliding against his skin. The gym was full of men working out, but Attlad went over to a quiet corner and traced out the boundaries of their court with a piece of charcoal.

It occurred to Micah as he watched that Attlad would not be using the formal thrust and parry system that he had been taught. This was not an exhibition for the benefit of students. Attlad was a soldier, used to real battles. Micah would be expected to fight as if his life depended on it. How far would Attlad go to test his mettle?

Attlad attacked without warning. Almost thrown by the unorthodox approach, Micah fell back into his defensive stance and then began to circle, keeping an eye out for any feint on Attlad's part. He wanted to observe for as long as possible, to get a feel for the man's rough style. What it lacked in elegance, it more than made up for in strength and deadly accuracy. Micah was thankful for the leather clothing that gave him at least some protection.

Several times Micah was forced to his knees, but as he became better acquainted with Attlad's crude style, he got better at defending himself. Now he began to attack from time to time, something Attlad had evidently not expected. By now, there was quite a crowd around them, fascinated by Micah's lightness and agility. But in the end, Attlad got the better of him and disarmed him with a totally unexpected and, in Micah's view, quite unfair move. He had to remind himself that there is no such thing as fair play on the battlefield. He was lucky his master didn't press his advantage and do him any physical harm.

When it was over, the others applauded, and Attlad handed the sword back to him.

"It's yours," he signed. "You earned it."

Micah thrust the sword into his belt and smiled his thanks. He was relieved that Attlad had won, in spite of his best efforts. His master seemed pleased with the whole performance, too. He beckoned to Micah to follow, and led the way out to the terrace where Micah had been kicked down the stairs days before.

Attlad and several of his men gathered around the table and a servant appeared with a jug of wine. Unsure what was expected of him, Micah took his place behind his master's chair. He felt that there was a slight difference in their relationship, now, though he couldn't find words to describe what had actually changed. Micah was still the slave, and he was reminded of it every time the rough leather of the tunic rubbed against the rings in his nipples. But there was a new respect between them. He realized with a glow of pleasure that Attlad was proud of him.

His master pointed to the ground and Micah knelt at his feet. The leggings made it awkward to separate his legs in the usual manner, but he knelt quickly, trying to accommodate himself to the new situation. He sipped the wine from Attlad's cup and then watched the flying hand signals in disbelief.

"We want you to take charge of the early training of the young ones," Attlad said.

Micah stared at him. "I am a slave," he said hesitantly.

"You have been trained as a Nebula Warrior. You can teach us their skills." Attlad slid his hand under Micah's tunic and his fingers moved on his slave's smooth chest. "I need you," they said.

Micah looked up into those clear grey eyes. "Yes, master." He would keep his questions till later, when they were alone.

When it was time for lunch, Micah went back to Attlad's apartment and took off his clothes. He felt more at ease naked, in these familiar surroundings. Attlad carried his bowl out to the terrace and set it on the table, beside his own. Micah looked at him questioningly, then climbed up on the table and crouched on all fours, his smooth ass raised to the sun.

"Eat!"

Obediently, Micah lowered his head to his bowl.

Attlad slipped his arm between his slave's legs and fingered the tear drop that hung there. Micah couldn't stop the moan that escaped him, but he went on eating. He spread himself to accommodate his master's hand. But Attlad was preoccupied, and presently he turned to his own food and left his slave alone. When he had finished eating, he fed Micah some bits of fruit from his own plate.

Kneeling on the table in front of him, Micah raised his hands. "Please, master. May I ask a question?"

"Ask."

"Will the boys pay any attention to a slave teacher?"

"If they do not, they will be punished."

"Will I be permitted to wear clothing?"

"The tunic and leggings, as you did this morning. It is for protection, only. That is all it means. After class, you will return here and take them off at once. Do you understand?"

"Yes, master. When does this begin?"

"This afternoon. Stop talking, now, and get down here."

At once, Micah scrambled off the table and knelt between his master's knees. He could see the erection straining against the fly of his pants, and he struggled with the buttons until at last it was free. Then Attlad took his slave's hands and locked them behind his back, so that Micah could touch him only with his mouth. As Attlad lay back, he hooked one leg over the arm of his chair to make himself more accessible to his slave. Micah rested his face against the coarse black hair surrounding his master's erect cock and nuzzled underneath, up under the heavy balls. He began to lick them gently all over, taking them inside his mouth and bathing them with his tongue. His master was pushing his hips forward, now, and Micah took the cue to move up to the straining cock. He tongued the length of it underneath, nibbled at the tip, letting his sharp teeth graze it, twisted his tongue around and around the shaft until Attlad grasped him by the hair and forced himself deep inside his slave's eager mouth. Micah's face went bright red as he was filled with his master's flesh, but he forced himself not to draw back, working his throat muscles strongly to give Attlad pleasure. When he came, Micah swallowed him and sat without moving, tonguing the throbbing penis as it faded, until Attlad withdrew.

The master looked down at the slave, noted the erection, and smiled. He extended his booted leg. "Find your release here," he said, pointing.

Micah straddled the boot at once and began rubbing himself against the smooth leather. Attlad reached lazily for the ring on his right nipple. As he twisted it, Micah came, with a cry. His seed shone against the black leather. Panting, Micah wiped it off with his long hair.

Satisfied, Attlad gave him the sign to get dressed. It was time to give his first lesson to the boys.

This time, when Attlad and his slave arrived at the gym, there were about a dozen boys sitting on benches at one end. With a jolt, Micah recognized the four who had humiliated him down by the river. He felt his face flush. How would he be able to control them if Attlad left? His master was making a speech and the boys were all listening respectfully. Then, Attlad gestured to Micah, handed him the sword and left the room.

The boys began to titter. They poked each other in the ribs. Some scratched at their crotches. Some were more forthright and made frankly sexual gestures towards Micah, who stood on a small platform in front of them, ready to demonstrate the twelve positions. He went through the first three, then stopped. The boy who had been the ringleader down by the river, had his pants open and was leering up at him.

Micah pointed to him. "Can you repeat what I just did?"

The whole class erupted in laughter and turned to watch, expectantly.

The boy spread his legs and gestured. "Fuck you."

"You are good at fucking, but not at fighting, is that what you're telling me?" Micah's anger was threatening to make him lose control.

The others had calmed down and were waiting for the response.

The boy hesitated. "I can fight," he gestured defiantly.

"Do what I just did." Micah held out the wooden practice sword.

The boy couldn't resist the direct challenge. He did up his pants and got to his feet. He sauntered up to the front. "Show me," he signed.

Micah repeated the three actions.

The boy laughed. "That's easy," he said, but he was not able to keep his balance and by the third gesture, he was lost. Puzzled, the boy looked at Micah. "Show me again," he commanded.

Now that he had everyone's undivided attention, Micah went through the positions more slowly. When the boy tried again, Micah guided his arm, corrected his posture, until at last he finished the first three positions correctly. The others cheered. Then they took up their positions, each armed with his own wooden sword, and began to practice the first three moves. They were still at it when Attlad arrived an hour later to rescue his slave.

"You have done well," he told him. "Go, now."

Micah had started down the corridor back to his master's room when he heard someone behind him. It was the boy from the river.

"What is your name?" Micah asked.

"Lin." There was a pause. The boy raised his hands uncertainly, as if not sure how to go on. "You are good," he said at last. "Is it true you were a Nebula Warrior?"

Micah nodded.

"And you will teach us all you know?"

"If that is Attlad's pleasure," Micah said.

"I wish you were my slave." Lin grinned at him knowingly. He touched Micah's hair but made no move towards anything more familiar. "See you tomorrow," he said, and ran off down the hall to rejoin his companions.

Micah breathed a sigh of relief. There would be no more trouble in class from that quarter. After class, perhaps, but he could take care of that.

Micah's days began to fall into another pattern. He still ran in the fields in the morning, still urged on with the whip held by Kee or Simon. When it was Kee, the whip stung his bare back and thighs more often and more deeply, but Micah gritted his teeth and kept on going. Attlad would often ride by and pick him up after this, and he learned to catch his master's strong hand as he galloped by and leap into the saddle in front of him. They would ride for a time like this until Attlad slowed the horse to a canter and caressed his slave into release. Once, Attlad undid his pants and lifted Micah's hips until he was impaled on his master's cock. Micah leaned forward, his arms clinging to the horse's rough neck as the animal's jolting canter made his master explode inside Micah with a shout.

Later, they would usually go back to the field and Micah would practice leaping from one horse to another, a feat he found terrifying and extremely difficult.

After lunch, which he still ate on the floor by Attlad's side, he went back to the apartment and got dressed for his class. The boys all paid attention, now. If they didn't, Lin would shout at them and bring them back into line. He was Micah's star pupil, and after class, he would often walk back with him to Attlad's apartment. Usually, he would make some provocative comment just before he left. "I'm jealous of your master," he would say. "I hope some day he will reward me for all my good work by giving me a few hours alone with you." Although he never went any further, Micah's uneasiness grew.

Then one day, Lin was still there when he came out of Attlad's apartment. He had never waited before. The boy's gaze lingered on Micah's nakedness, his eyes bright. He licked his lips.

"Why are you still here?" Micah asked. All his instincts told him to retreat, but he couldn't back away in front of the boy.

"Where are you going now?" Lin asked, ignoring the question.

"To the courtyard terrace for a drink of protein."

"I'll come with you."

"Attlad might not like you there," Micah said.

"Attlad has gone hunting," Lin said with satisfaction.

Micah was in no position to order the boy away. He strode quickly along the corridor, feeling the boy's eyes on him. At times, Lin was so close his arm brushed Micah"s bare thigh. When they reached the terrace, Kee was there, holding Micah's silver bottle. Micah's heart sank. He had been hoping to find Simon, instead.

Kee looked at the two of them and grinned his unpleasant smile. He pointed to the ground in front of him. Micah went down on his knees, resigned to being humiliated in front of his pupil. But Kee had sized up the situation better than Micah realized. He handed the bottle to Lin and withdrew to the shadows to watch.

It was obvious that Lin relished the idea of playing master to the beautiful blond man, if only for a few minutes. Micah hated Kee even more for this. He sensed dimly that Lin was being put at risk by Kee, but he couldn't figure out how. Lin planted himself in front of the kneeling Micah and thrust the bottle at him. Micah dropped his eyes as he sucked at the teat. At once he recognized the taste of the drug that was often given him as a tranquillizer. Why now? He looked over at Kee, standing smugly by the door, watching, and his unease increased. Lin stepped closer and rested a hand on his shoulder. Kee was trying to make trouble, that much was clear, but what exactly he had in mind, was not.

Micah pulled away from the bottle and shook his head. "I don't need any more," he signed to Lin. The boy put the bottle down at once but Kee shouted to him. He sprang out of the shadow and hit Micah a stinging blow across the face. He shouted again and Lin picked up the bottle.

"Drink it all," Kee signed.

Micah started to shake his head and Kee hit him again. Then he pulled off his belt and began to beat Micah on the shoulders, the back. He shouted at him but Micah couldn't understand the words. Only the tone was clear. Anger. Hatred. Frustration. Lin was watching, wide-eyed. The scene was obviously exciting him. Perhaps it was meant to. Kee ordered Micah to bend over the end of the table and beat his buttocks until they were hot. Then he kicked Micah's legs wider apart and said something to Lin.

Micah felt the boy's hands on his hips, shaking with excitement. Then Lin's cock pushed into his anus. While the boy pumped into him, Kee watched, pulling Micah's face up so he could see the tears that streaked his reddened face. When Lin came, Kee gathered a handful of Micah's long blond hair, pulled him up and flung him on the ground. Then he turned on his heel and walked away into the Complex.

Lin did up his pants and sat down on the ground beside Micah. His face was flushed. He didn't look at the naked man, but concentrated on pulling up tufts of grass with his brown hands.

Once Micah had control of his breathing again, he touched Lin's arm to get his attention. "Kee will tell Attlad," he said. "He will try to get you in trouble for this."

"I shouldn't have done it," Lin said. "What will I do now?"

"Tell him yourself."

"He will believe me?"

"I think so. He knows Kee."

Lin thought for a moment. "I will," he said. He got to his feet. At the door, he paused and clapped his hands to make sure Micah was paying attention. "I'm sorry," he signed.

Micah nodded. After a few moments, he too got up and went into the Complex. He would wait for his master in his apartment.

When Attlad came back from the hunt, he stretched his legs for Micah to take off his boots. Obediently, Micah turned his back to his master, straddled the boot and pulled. Attlad held out his other foot and once again Micah pulled off the boot. This time, his foot stayed between Micah's legs, nudging his genitals, rubbing against the gold ring and its red tear drop. He turned his slave around to face him and smiled to see the red and blue dragon stretch towards him eagerly along Micah's erect penis.

"You had trouble with Kee today?" he asked, idly stroking him.

Micah nodded, his breath coming faster.

A moment later, Kee himself came into the room and bowed before Attlad. He paid no attention to Micah who stood between Attlad's legs.

"Chento needs release," Attlad said. "He has earned a reward."

"Sir?"

"Take off your pants and present yourself to be fucked."

Kee expostulated, then pleaded, but without avail. Attlad's grey eyes had gone cold as ice. With hands trembling with anger and humiliation, Kee pulled down his pants and stepped out of them. Attlad pointed to the table and the servant unwillingly bent over, as Attlad instructed him to.

"Take him, Chento."

Micah hesitated. It was tempting, but was it what he really wanted? He raised his hands to signal. "Being fucked is not a punishment, is it?" he asked. "It will give him pleasure."

Attlad seemed to consider the idea. Then he shook his head. "Not when the man doing it is you, Chento. There are other things you can do to him, of course. The choice is up to you. Ask yourself, will the act give you pleasure?"

Micah looked over to where Kee's bare ass was raised invitingly towards him. It would be humiliating for this man to be fucked by a slave, especially one he hated. Micah felt a great sense of elation sweep through him as he walked over and grasped Kee's hips. He positioned his cock just at the opening of Kee's asshole, braced his knees and thrust himself all the way inside. Kee cried out once. Micah thrust deeply over and over, relishing the shudders and suppressed moans he felt in the man under him. From time to time he paused, wanting to make this humiliation last as long as possible for the man who hated him so much.

He reache d around Kee's waist and felt for his cock. Kee started to push his hand away but at a sound from Attlad, he stopped. Micah smiled with triumph to feel the cock hard, and squeezed and twisted it savagely. Kee groaned. Satisfied, Micah concentrated on his own release. When it was over, he waited for a few moments, before he withdrew and watched his come drip down the man's leg.

Slowly, Kee straightened up. Without a word, he stepped into his pants, forcing his still hard cock inside before doing them up. He didn't raise his eyes. There was no sound in the room but his laboured breathing.

Micah glanced at Attlad and smiled. Revenge was very sweet.

NINE

ttlad lay on his back in the grass on his private terrace, while his slave licked gravy off his flat, hard stomach. It was noon. The sun was hot on Micah's back and the muscles of his buttocks and thighs stood out as he worked. His master's naked body gleamed where Micah's tongue had licked him, his chest, his stomach, his crotch. Micah stuck his tongue into the thick black pubic hair, getting the last of the gravy from the lunch he had eaten off Attlad's warm body. It was a turn-on the like of which he had never experienced before. His master's imagination knew no bounds, it seemed.

When there was no speck of food left anywhere, Micah began to suck on the man's long hard nipples until Attlad pushed him onto his stomach and entered him. When he had come, Attlad didn't withdraw. Micah lay under him, drifting off to sleep, warmed by the sun and his master's solid body, his master's cock still up his ass. At length he became aware of Attlad's fingers moving over his shoulder. Micah concentrated on the signs, hearing Attlad's words as if he had spoken them.

"You give me much pleasure," Attlad let him know. "But do you hold something back?"

"Nothing, master!"

"Do you give me everything?"

"My whole being!" He wanted to say, my soul, but didn't know the sign for such a concept. Micah searched in his mind for some way to convince Attlad of his complete devotion. "I would give you my life!"

"Would you give me your sight?"

"Yes."

"Your hearing?"

"Yes." Micah agreed to everything Attlad asked of him, but he felt a cold shiver, knowing these were not idle thoughts. Attlad was serious. He was demanding a final sign of submission. "I give you whatever you wish to take, master," Micah said.

"Soon we will go on a mission, you and I," Attlad told him. Micah lay with his head on Attlad's crotch, his long hair spilled over on the grass, watching his master's hands tell him about the mission.

Micah knew of the arrangement by which his home planet kept control of Earth Base Gamma 1. The agreement of non-interference was ratified every five years, and it was time. Attlad and Sar had been chosen to sign for the Kudites, but there was unrest in the nation about the recent Terran uprisings. There had been more recon planes brought down, all of which had strayed far from the accepted air space around the Base. The Kudites did not trust their smooth-talking sometime allies from a distant world.

"How important is their station to them, Chento?" Attlad asked him.

"It is a refuelling station, a stopover on long flights."

"That is all? What of the colony?"

"It isn't working out. There were supposed to be good prospects for mining, but the desert around the Base is too difficult to work in. It's too expensive to keep the mine running and the colonists keep striking for higher pay because of all the risks."

Attlad nodded thoughtfully. He kissed Micah on the mouth. "Come. Sar is waiting to talk."

Attlad showered and dressed in a fine black tunic and leggings and shiny black boots. Micah brushed his long blond hair and submitted patiently while Simon was called in to paint a blue and gold band high on his forehead. Attlad handed him the blue leather collar and the bracelets for his ankles and wrists. Then he led the way down to the main courtyard.

Musicians played softly high in a gallery overlooking the courtyard. Servants hurried back and forth carrying wine and fruit and other delicacies Micah didn't have words for. He smiled when he saw Sar with his beautiful brown eyed slave squatting between his legs. The boy smiled back at him shyly.

Sar and Attlad spoke together using hand signs so that Micah and the boy could follow them. From time to time, Attlad would question Micah on some point concerning the Base.

"I was there so short a time, master," Micah told him. "I didn't get to know that much."

"But you can access their files? Check the records in their computer machines?"

"I have the knowledge, yes, master."

As Micah continued to follow the rest of the discussion, he felt a flutter of panic. What would it be like to return to Base 1 as a Kudite love slave? How would they see him? He glanced at the boy, but his eyes were fixed, as ever, on his master. Of course, it would not be the same for him. He was not a Terran. It would be an alien world to him. And to me? he wondered. This, he realized, would be the toughest test of all.

When the two leaders finished their business, they turned to more pleasant topics of conversations. Attlad slipped a finger inside Micah's ass as he talked and at once, his slave hardened. Sar noticed and laughed. He said something and patted his boy on the arm. Attlad nodded. He turned to Micah.

"You have been watching Sar's slave with interest," he signed. "It is our pleasure to see you two couple on the grass."

Micah glanced over and saw Sar ordering the boy onto his back. He lay down at once, opening his slender smooth thighs for Micah and raising his hands above his head submissively, obviously the way he had been taught.

Micah found the boy very attractive, his long delicate limbs, the high muscular buttocks, the black wiry hair between his legs where the gold ring winked. As Micah knelt over him, the boy raised his hips and wrapped his legs around Micah's waist, wriggling himself into position expertly so that his hole was open and ready.

"You are really something," Micah murmured.

The boy's hands moved at once. "I cannot hear you," he said. "I gave my hearing to my master."

Micah stared down at him, wondering if he had understood. He remembered the intense attention the boy always paid. With a shock, he saw the reason.

Micah had intended to be slow and gentle, but the two masters had other ideas. Just as Micah was about to enter the boy, Attlad slapped his ass hard. He kept on hitting him with the flat of his hand and Micah thrust abruptly into the boy in a reflex action, pumping hard and fast. Sar meanwhile, reached between the two and pulled on the boy's rings until he began to suck at Micah's nipples frantically. The hard rhythmic slaps of Attlad's hand bounced off the stone walls of the courtyard, making an odd counterpoint to the slap of Micah's naked flesh against the boy's ass. Micah felt the boy's cock jerk spasmodically and he cried out just before Micah came and Attlad at last stopped hitting him.

Neither one of them moved, waiting for a signal from their masters. When it came, the boy crawled over to Sar and sipped wine from his glass. Micah laid his head against Attlad's thigh and caught his breath. His face was red and streaked with sweat and tears.

That night, after eating his dinner from the bowl on the floor beside his master in the dining hall, Attlad led him outside and up the hill to a small glade of trees. He had brought a leather satchel with him which he set down on the ground. Micah knelt before him, trying to see his face clearly in the pale moonlight.

"Tomorrow we go to the Earth Base, Gamma 1," Attlad said. "Are you ready?"

"Yes, master."

"You will give me your final gift tonight," he went on. "What will it be?"

"My hearing, master, if that pleases you."

"It pleases me very much. Come closer."

Micah knelt upright before his master and Attlad opened the satchel and took out a square black box affair with wires dangling from it. Then he fitted what looked like a set of headphones over his ears. Everything grew muffled. When he attached them to the wires from the box, there was a flash of light, followed by blinding pain.

Micah screamed.

Attlad held him against his strong body and after a

while, Micah realized he no longer wore the ear phones. He couldn't hear a thing. There was no sighing of the breeze in the trees, no distant murmur from the open windows of the complex, no sleepy twittering of birds. He clung desperately to Attlad, feeling disoriented and afraid. He could feel his master's breath against his ear, but he heard nothing. He pushed one hand under Attlad's tunic.

"I am afraid!" he signed rapidly. His teeth were chattering and he shivered convulsively.

"You are with me," Attlad told him, his fingers moving over Micah's face. "You are part of me."

Calmed by his master's words and gestures, Micah held Attlad's hand and followed him back down the hill and in through the hall to their apartment. Micah felt totally exhausted. The pain still buzzed in his head. Attlad undressed and took him to bed. He caressed him and made love to him, with a gentleness he had never exhibited before. When Micah cried, Attlad licked away the tears, holding his slave in his strong arms. At last Micah turned to him, brimming over with love, and devoured his skin with his tongue. He licked every bit of his master's beautiful muscled body, thrusting his tongue deep inside him, matting the dark hair on his ass with his spital. He filled his mouth with his master's cock and drank him dry over and over again. He was in a frenzy of devotion, only calming when Attlad slapped his face with his bare hand several times and threw him on his stomach. He tied his hands to the rod at the top of the bed and thrust a leather dildo up his ass. Micah felt stuffed, filled, replete. Attlad left him like that, his anus stretched wide to accommodate the long thick leather shaft, and at last, Micah fell asleep to his soundless dreaming.

Micah woke up with a gentle breeze caressing his warm skin. His hands were freed from the restraints. He lay on his side and looked out the open door to the terrace where he could see Attlad looking over some papers. Then he heard a bell.

Micah sat up so abruptly he felt dizzy for a moment. The far off call of the bell came to him through the door, sharp and clear. Then he heard other sounds. His master's exclamation of annoyance. The hum from the air circulator. The creak of the bed as he moved.

"I don't understand," he murmured, and he heard his own voice, not deep within his head but real, true, clear.

Micah walked onto the terrace and knelt at his master's feet. He touched his forehead to Attlad's booted foot and washed the black leather with his tears. "You gave it back!" he sobbed. "You gave my hearing back to me! How?"

Attlad pulled his hair until his face was tilted up towards him. "I need you," Attlad said. "I need all your faculties for this mission."

"I understand."

"Last night was only a temporary deafness. All that was necessary was that you freely gave yourself to me."

"It was a test?"

"In a way. Of course, I may claim it back at any time. Permanently. Like Sar did."

"Yes, master."

The rest of the day passed as usual, except there was an air of expectation, of movement and preparation everywhere. Even though Micah was not a part of it, he was aware of what was going on. The men were preoccupied. Even Simon appeared to have his mind on other things besides his master's favoured slave. In the arms class, the boys were restless. They wanted to ask questions about the Base, but Micah was uneasy. He didn't know how much he was supposed to divulge of the plans. He parried their questions or feigned ignorance.

Attlad did not summon him for dinner and Micah crouched over his bowl of stew alone in his master's apartment. He was thinking of the mission. He was very apprehensive, knowing he would face scorn, disbelief, laughter. A Nebula Warrior who been become a sex slave is a rare thing. A pitiable thing to some, he knew. It would take great strength and determination to cleave to his purpose and serve his master well under these conditions.

When Attlad appeared, he looked worried. Micah had never seen him that strained before. The tension was in his eyes. Alarmed, Micah went to him and helped take off his heavy riding boots. Then Attlad fell back in his chair.

"Chento, my father has summoned you to him."

The one with the visions. The soothsayer. Micah shivered.

"I don't want to do this, but I have no choice, do you understand?"

"Yes master." Micah understood. He remembered his own father, who had died five years ago. He remembered how he strove to meet those exacting standards, what a strain it was when he made a decision he knew his father would not approve of. Even a leader, his master, would have these feelings.

Attlad reached out for Micah and pulled his head against him for a moment, his hands caressing the long hair. Then he pushed him away. "Make yourself ready for him. There is no time for formal grooming."

Micah went to the mirror and brushed his hair. He slipped the blue bracelets on his wrists, on his ankles. There was still a pale blue band high on his forehead. He could see Attlad's reflection as his master stood behind him, watching. Attlad opened a small tube of paste and rubbed it into Micah's hard nipples until they glistened and shone with a deeper colour. As he moved, they caught the light and sparkled. Attlad opened his legs, separated his buttocks. He rubbed the glistening frosted oil on his asshole.

"Go. Simon will show you the way."

"Yes, master."

Micah followed the servant through the by now familiar corridors and through a door into an elevator. This was new. He had not realized there were such things as elevators in the deliberately primitive building. They rose silently through the inner core of the Complex built into the rocks and emerged at last somewhere near the top. The doors opened and Simon pushed him out. With a soft whisper, the doors closed behind him, leaving him on his own.

It was cooler than usual up here and Micah shivered, feeling the goose bumps break out on his naked skin. By the dim lighting, he could see rough black walls that looked as if they had been recently dug out of the cliff that was their home. They glinted dully. Some mineral, perhaps, Micah thought. He went forward towards the sound of running water. The light grew gradually brighter until he came to a large open room with a dazzling sheet of water cascading down one wall. A young man stood in the waterfall with his arms raised. He was naked and his long hair cascaded down his back. He appeared to be dancing. If he saw Micah, he gave no sign and the slave passed on to the next room, which was filled with a fragrant blue smoke.

An old man sat on a canopied couch at one end of this room, wrapped in a colourful silk robe. In front of him was a large elaborate urn, with several attachments. Micah realized it was the source of the smoke. The man was perfectly bald. A silver braided headband circled his brow.

Micah walked over to him and knelt down. He raised his hands to announce who he was. "I am Chento. My master sent me."

"I know who you are." The man's signs were hard to read

at first, but Micah soon figured out most of it. "My son did not want to send you to me, did he?" Micah thought it prudent not to answer this, and the man went on: "Stand up and show me what my stubborn son is so enamoured of."

Micah got to his feet at once and moved closer to the old man. For some reason he didn't understand, the scrutiny of those milky eyes made him uneasy. It was as though this were the first time he had stood naked in front of anyone, and he felt a deep flush spread over his cheeks. The old man reached out a freckled brown hand and touched his cock. He pulled it lightly.

"My son has put his mark on you everywhere, I see," he said with a smile. "Not that I blame him. Here. Sit beside me." He patted the couch at his side and Micah sat down. The old man's hand touched his nipples, moving from the right to left and back again. Then he pushed Micah gently back against the pillows and fiddled with the strange complicated pipe on the low table. The old man inserted one of the smooth tubes in Micah's mouth and instructed him to draw on it deeply. For long moments, Micah lay back on the pillows and drank in the heavy sweet smoke from the pipe. He had expected to cough or have some trouble, since he was not used to it, but nothing happened. Just a gentle languor softening his bones so that it became difficult to feel the outer limits of his body. Where did he end, the pillows begin?

From this reclining position, he could see the entrance to the room where the slender young boy from the fountain now appeared, dressed in a loose flowing gown. His hair was long and gleamed deep red in the dim light, a colour that seemed not quite natural to Micah. The old man beckoned to him. The boy was closer, now, moving with a fluid grace. The light shone clearly on the finely chiselled face, the choker of pearls about his neck. The fine spun material of the gown hung loosely from his shoulders, and as he moved, it opened, revealing small, pointed breasts.

"A girl?" Micah murmured.

The old man smiled lazily. His hand caressed the girl's soft thigh. "Play for us, my dear."

The girl drifted off and picked up a stringed instrument and soon soft music filled the room. Was it the smoke that sang so sweetly?

"Would you like to lie with my young one?" asked the old man.

Micah knew he should say no. Say that he was Attlad's and wanted only what his master wanted. But he found he was unable to say this. His hand moved slowly, so slowly and he said, "Yes, sir. I am...curious."

The old man smiled. His milky eyes swam in the air above Micah. It was odd that his vision seemed so unsure, so lacking in depth, while his hearing was as keen and acute as ever. Another odd thing was how he seemed to hear the words, yet he knew the old man could not speak his language, was moving his hands and signing, just as his master did.

"If you knew a great cataclysm would demolish the Earth Base Gamma 1, would you warn your people?"

"My people?" Micah blinked. "I don't know what you mean."

"Answer my question."

"I...I don't want anyone to get hurt, sir."

"Let me ask you this. If Attlad gave you the order to pull the lever that would destroy them, would you do it?"

Micah felt a great shout of denial rising through him, a final faint memory of the oath he had taken to hold true to the government and people of his home planet, but another part of him saw only his master, and the order he had given. "I would do what Attlad commanded," he told the old man, and took another long draw on the pipe.

"What is the name of the commander of the Base?"

"Harlon Williams, sir."

"What do you know about him?"

"He is the man who was sent in to make things right again. A troubleshooter. He has great skill in diplomacy but he can be ruthless. At least, that is what it said in the reports. I have not met him. He came just after I…left."

"Is he a married man?"

"Yes, sir. His wife was not coming with him, apparently."

"Would he be interested in you?"

"No, sir. Not at all in the way you mean."

"Again according to the reports." Micah nodded. "And that sort of thing would be in the reports?"

"Oh, yes, sir. Everything is in the reports. Sexual orientation, favourite food. Everything."

"How did you come to read them?"

"I had clearance. I knew the system and how to access the confidential files. And I was…curious."

"I see."

Micah felt that he was floating, now. The music was under his skin, running like ice water through his veins and throbbing between his legs. He moved restlessly and became aware of the girl with the long red hair, lying naked beside him. Micah raised himself with difficulty and looked down at her. He covered one of the soft pointed breasts with one hand. With the other hand, he explored between the slender legs, and found a small but definite cock.

"What are you?" he asked.

"Whatever you want me to be."

"I want…I want…" But he had lost the thread. He no longer knew what he wanted. He heard laughter and saw the boy's mouth open. Micah blinked and saw a red field dotted with blue flowers. Inside him a tide was rising, his desire fed by the hard boy hands, rising without his knowl-edge or understanding. He arched his back into the pillows, his legs spread wide to accommodate the boy with the pearls and the willing mouth.

And Micah knew what he wanted.

"Attlad!"

TEN

ands were shaking Micah. Pinching him. Slapping his face. Micah opened his eyes and hit out at his attackers, surprised that he was not in restraints. He threw one man to the ground and kicked out viciously at another, driving him back.

"Chento!"

"Attlad?"

Micah squinted in the bright lights of the corridor. He realized he was outside the old man's private elevator but he couldn't remember how he had gotten there. Numbly he reached out to his master. Attlad knocked his hand away. The other men were servants, wearing the red tunics of handlers, but he didn't recognize them.

Attlad waved them away and when they had gone, he turned Micah around, bent him over and told him to spread his ass. Micah almost fell as he tried to present himself for Attlad's inspection. He still felt dizzy and strangely weak. He couldn't understand why his master should be so angry with him that he twisted his fingers inside until Micah fell against the wall for support.

Attlad pulled him upright and reached out for his cock. He lifted it and attacked a clip to the ring and tugged at it. He led his slave back along the familiar corridors by the ring in his now erect member until they came to his own apartment. Casually he hung the loop of the narrow leash over the doorknob and told Micah to stay.

Micah leaned against the door feebly. The leash would not allow him to sit or kneel on the floor without pulling at his cock unmercifully and he watched Attlad hurry away with a mounting sense of anxiety and confusion. What have I done? he asked himself, and it worried him that he could not remember. Had he betrayed his master? Servants hurried by. Several grooms. A few handlers. Some of them glanced at him with curiosity. Some laughed when they saw his plight. Mostly they ignored him.

After a while, Micah unhooked the leash from the door handle and sank to the ground to rest. His limbs were shaking and he knew he would have fallen if he had tried to stay on his feet much longer. He knew he would be punished, but at the moment, he refused to worry.

Attlad said nothing when he returned. He picked up the lead and pulled him inside with it. Micah bit his lip to keep from crying out as the pain tore into his cock. He started to explain that he had a dizzy spell but Attlad pointed to the foot of the bed. Micah lay down. In spite of the pain between his legs, he drifted off to sleep almost at once.

When he woke up, his mind was clear. His memory of the night with Attlad's father was still very indistinct, but now he realized that he had been given some sort of drug. A truth drug. The anxiety about whether or not he had betrayed his master was gone. It occurred to him that Attlad was angry because he didn't know what had gone on between Micah and his father and he was too proud to ask his slave for any details.

Kee was in the room, packing a wicker box with papers and a few notebooks and writing materials. Attlad was sitting at the table going over a list with another man. Micah sat up alertly. Were they about to leave? He felt a sick feeling in the pit of his stomach. When Kee saw Micah was awake, he brought a silver bottle over at once and presented it. His expression was carefully neutral. Micah made him hold it for a moment before he took the teat in his mouth. The cool thick liquid tasted good to him and he drank it thirstily, pausing in between gulps to make Kee stand beside him patiently a little longer until he was finished. He wondered if Attlad knew how often Kee had tired of the job and pulled the food away from Micah's hungry lips. Micah knew Kee would do whatever he could to hurt him the first time he thought he could get away with it.

Simon appeared soon afterwards and led Micah away to the grooming room. The big man appeared sad as he washed Micah carefully with the spray, shaved his body, dried him and rubbed the familiar scented oil into his skin. His hands lingered this time, much more than before. His fingers outlined the muscles on Micah's chest, caressed the inside of Micah's thighs, and gently cupped his balls. At last, Micah caught Simon's hand.

"What is it?" he asked.

"You will be leaving soon," Simon said.

"I will be back."

"No. Attlad will take you with him to the Citadel when you leave the Terran Base."

"And you?"

"I stay here. I am not a soldier. I am part of the Complex."

"Have you been to the Citadel?"

"Yes. It is a huge city dug into the great canyons on the

other side of the desert. Only a small part of it is above the ground. Things are much more rigid there. Life is…tense."

"The life of a slave?"

"Turn over."

Micah turned on his stomach. Since he could no longer see Simon's hands, they could no longer talk. He mulled over what he had been told, and what he had not been told, and the butterflies woke up in his stomach.

They were to travel to the Station in the long distance Carrier that was stored on top of the complex. Micah had heard about these huge machines. He knew, too, that the Kudites allowed no private flyers of any sort. The carriers were only used for group transport over a long distance. Each Complex had one, and they were capable of carrying the horses, which were the preferred mode of travel.

That afternoon, Micah walked with the group of Kudites up onto the roof of the building and watched with interest as the giant aircraft was lifted up through the roof and settled on the landing pad. It was an awkward craft by Micah's standards, but it was sturdy and serviceable. It would get them there.

Micah walked up the gangplank behind Attlad and followed his master to a row of cubicles where he was told to wait. They were stacked one above the other. Micah crawled onto the shelf his master pointed to and Attlad closed the transparent door, shutting him in the small space. He felt panic for a moment, shut up naked in this box that was nothing more than a glorified bunk. Through his door, he could see others milling about, pausing to peer in at him. They grinned or frowned in annoyance, obviously trying to find their own cubicles. Micah wondered how long he would have to stay here and if Attlad would join him. There hardly seemed room for two of them. Then there was a click as the doors locked, followed by the loud throbbing hum of the engines starting up. The huge craft began to move sedately into the air.

It shouldn't take long to get there, even at this ridiculously low speed, Micah thought. About half an hour later, a servant came to let him out and take him to Attlad. His master was alone in the small cabin. He stood by the wicker box they had brought with them, leafing through the papers there, a worried frown on his face.

"We need to know their estimate of our strength," he said. His hands moved but he didn't look at Micah. "We have to know what information they have about us."

"But master, how can I...I didn't realize this is what you wanted from me."

Attlad stared into his eyes. "You are having second thoughts."

"No! I...I just don't know how—"

"You have made your choice, Chento. Together we will find a way. Put this on."

Attlad handed him a beautiful collar of gold, with blue gems set around it, and a large flat tear shaped ruby in the middle.

"Is this all I am to wear?" Micah asked, suddenly feeling weak at the prospect of walking naked among these men and women he had worked with.

"You are my love slave. It is all you need."

Micah fastened the collar around his neck. There was a loop at the back, he noted, for a chain or a leash. Suddenly Attlad wrapped a fistful of Micah's hair around one hand and pulled his face close.

"I have laid my life in your hands, every bit as much as you laid yours in mine. Remember that."

Micah swallowed his heart. He had no words. He turned his head and kissed his master's hand.

He felt the great craft shudder as it slowed and finally

came to rest outside the huge protective bubble of the Earth Base Gamma 1. Attlad attached a thin blue leather lead to the loop of Micah's collar and hooked the other end into his own belt.

"We are ready," he said.

They joined Sar and the other richly dressed Kudite men who formed their party. Micah noticed Sar's young slave was not with them. Was this to put the spotlight on him? Was he to be flaunted as the focus of all eyes, obviously a Terran, one of them reduced to the status of a naked sex slave? There were horses waiting for them there and the Kudite leaders mounted. Micah ran along beside his master's horse, head high, arms locked behind his back, as he had done so often around the field outside the complex. The company advanced down the ramp into the evening sun, their banners flying.

Micah felt as if he were seeing the Station for the first time. Everything looked so familiar, yet completely different. There must have been quite a campaign to clean up after the riots. New paint gleamed everywhere and new structures now towered where before there were nothing but burnt out ruins. They entered the Station through a long enclosed tunnel. The horses shied as the air changed, and the atmosphere became more moist and cool. The Terran welcoming party was on foot. Micah recognized two of the men as high ranking officers. At once he reached up and laid his hand on Attlad's thigh and told him what he knew about them. When he stopped, Attlad caressed him briefly with his fingers.

"Welcome to Earth Base Gamma 1!" exclaimed Lieutenant Frazier, a wide smile on his handsome tanned face. His white hair rose in disciplined waves over his forehead.

The Kudites drew together in a line and dismounted.

Micah stood beside his master, watching the Terrans warily. This was the moment he had been dreading, the first time he saw that look of shock and contempt in their eyes. It was on Frazier's face when he glanced at Micah and saw his nakedness. For a moment, his expression froze, then he looked away.

Nex was translating the polite message of welcome while the two groups looked each other over.

"The Commander is waiting for you in the Reception Hall," Frazier said. "We were not expecting so many of you," he added. His eyes slid to Micah and then away.

"The servants need not come," Sar told him, through Nex.

Frazier bowed and led the way onto the moving sidewalk. The street was lined with curious citizens, waiting to see the famous barbarians. The exotic love slave was their main interest. Men and women, girls and boys, all craned their necks to see the oiled perfection of his naked body. Micah couldn't help hearing the exclamation and comments as they passed.

"Look at the blond hair! That's no Kudite!"

"They don't know any shame."

"Isn't that guy cold, mom?"

"Hush! Get back in the house!"

How pale they all looked. Even the guards they passed here and there seemed out of shape to Micah, compared to the Kudites. Let them gape. Did they understand that he was Attlad's most valuable possession? His treasure? That was why he was here, on exhibit. If they didn't know that, he did. Micah raised his chin proudly and looked straight ahead as they stepped off the moving sidewalk and entered the Commander's residence.

Micah had never been inside this grand building before. The public part was a long series of interlocking rooms where the Commander could entertain visiting dignitaries in large or small numbers. Huge satellite pictures of Earth and its colonies lined the hallway. In the reception area, portraits of past Commanders hung beside the portraits of other highly placed Terran officials. It was all very official, very formal.

The room was full of men and women in dress uniform, sipping wine and talking in hushed voices. Micah was aware of an audible gasp as he entered, slightly behind Attlad. The leash still attached them, a visible symbol of their relationship. Frazier introduced them to Commander Harlon Williams and several of his aides and advisors. They were all new since Micah had left, except for the Information Officer, Linda Dawson. She was having a lot of trouble dealing with Micah. She was so flustered, he knew it never occurred to her to question who he might be.

When Attlad was shown to a chair, Micah sank to the floor at his feet, his knees far apart, one hand on Attlad's thigh. He kept his ears open, very aware of the behind-the-hand comments that were not picked up by the official translators. 'Is he for real?' 'How come the guy has a male slave?' 'Wouldn't you, if he looked like that?' Those he thought pertinent, he passed on to Attlad. He found it exhausting, this constant monitoring of conversations, movements, meanings that were not spoken. But he knew he was picking up things the Kudites would otherwise miss. Now and then, he drank some wine from Attlad's proffered glass. Every time he moved he was aware of eyes on him, studying him covertly. He knew he caused acute embarrassment to some of the younger men and women. When he caught them looking at him, they blushed and looked away.

It was worse when they went into the great dinning hall. Here there was some confusion as to where Micah was to sit, but Attlad insisted on him being by his side and at last gave his permission for Micah to sit on the chair next to him. Micah found it strange sitting at a table after all this time, feeling the rough weave of the material of the chair seat against his bare ass. He was constantly glancing at his master, making sure it was all right to feed himself, to drink the wine on his own. Attlad appeared to ignore him, but under the table he had a hand on Micah's bare thigh, asking questions. Then he would turn his hand over and Micah would answer, his fingers on the palm of his master's hand.

The dinner was just getting underway, when Micah became aware of a someone staring at him. Hard. He waited until the Commander had finished speaking to the woman beside him before turning his head. He caught his breath and almost dropped the glass he held in one hand. For a moment, blood pounded in his ears and he heard nothing. Attlad's fingers digging into his leg, brought him back. Micah swallowed. He had never expected to see that face again. Those piercing blue eyes. Staring at him in disbelief. Royal!

"Chento!" At last, his master was speaking his name.

"It is my lover."

"No! I am your lover," Attlad retorted, his fingers digging at him angrily.

"I mean, he was. I thought he was dead."

"What is his rank? Is he important?" Attlad's fingers continued to intrude.

Not realizing what he was doing, Micah pushed the hand away. It was pain that brought him back to his senses. Attlad pulled at his genitals under the table. Micah shuddered and bowed his head, trying to collect himself.

Attlad repeated his question.

Micah looked again down the table where Royal sat beside another man who looked vaguely familiar. "He is an aid to the commander," he told Attlad. "Not very important." But it took him a while to pull his mind back to his job.

The Terrans were much more relaxed, now. Some of them looked at him openly, asking questions which Attlad parried carefully. It was obvious the idea of total control of one human being over another intrigued many of them.

"Do you mean he will do anything you ask?" Lieutenant Linda Dawson asked. Her face was flushed with wine and she had become quite outspoken as the dinner wore on.

"Perhaps you want a demonstration?" Attlad asked.

The Commander began to murmur against this, but Attlad stood up and pushed back the dishes and cutlery, making more space. "On the table, on your back," he ordered his slave.

Micah felt a great wave of panic as his master unhooked the lead from his collar. For one long moment, he thought he could not obey. Not here. Not in front of these people. He opened his mouth, closed it. He got up and turned around so he was sitting on the table. He lay back and swung his legs up and over, stretching out full length with his hands clasped together above his head. He heard Royal's voice above the other exclamations. "No, Micah! Don't!" Then he looked up at Attlad and moved his legs apart.

Attlad looked around the table. He picked up a candlestick and held it over Micah's prone nakedness. Without a change in his expression, he tipped the candle and dripped the hot molten wax on Micah's tender nipples. There were loud exclamations of protest from the onlookers. Micah gritted his teeth. He watched Attlad move the candle lower down, knowing the pain would strike again, this time at the tender skin of his groin.

"Stop!" cried the Commander.

Attlad tipped the candle. Micah caught his breath and set his jaw as the wax hit him just above the pubic hair. Attlad laid a possessive hand under his slave's genitals and smiled at the inevitable response. His symbol, the blue and red dragon, grew and swelled full length under his touch.

"This is power," he said. "And it is trust." He motioned Micah back to his seat.

"That is unbelievable," muttered Frazier.

"It's barbaric cruelty!" Micah didn't recognize the voice.

Micah sat quietly beside his master, glad he had not shamed Attlad by crying out or betraying the pain he was in. He felt the uneasiness around him. They could not cope well with the demonstration of a power he sensed fascinated most of them and shamed them. As the Commander rose to give an official end to the dinner, Attlad raised his hand.

"I wish to show my trust of Commander Williams, by giving him the gift of Chento, my slave, for the rest of he night, to do with as he wishes."

When this was translated, there was an appalled intake of breath from the assembly. Micah tensed. At once he saw what Attlad wanted him to do. But did he understand a man like the Commander? Micah was deeply afraid that his master had too much faith in the charms of his Terran slave. The Commander seemed to be having trouble understanding that the gesture was not just that, a gesture of good will. He conferred with his aide for a moment. Royal and another aide seemed to be urging him to accept.

Commander Williams faced his Kudite guest with great dignity. His face was grey and strained. Micah knew that he would be very concerned about causing any kind of misunderstanding at this point in the proceedings. He bowed slightly to Attlad.

"I accept your gesture of good will in the spirit in

which it was offered. I would, however, prefer to enjoy the young man's company tomorrow."

"Tomorrow is for business," Attlad said. "To night, is for pleasure."

ELEVEN

icah strode along the silent corridor like a warrior going into battle. He *was* a warrior, he reminded himself, although the guards would see only a naked slave, bought and paid for by an alien chief. The deep pile of the floor covering felt like grass under his feet. He wasn't absolutely sure where the Commander's sleeping quarters were, but he knew they would be wherever there were guards, and so far, he hadn't come across anyone but a frightened young maid who ran in terror when she saw him.

At last, he saw two men standing at ease near the end of the hall. He wondered if either of them had been on the Base when he was an officer here. After a moment's hesitation, he decided to keep going until they stopped him.

"Sorry. Out of bounds," the taller one said. His expression was hidden by the jutting mouthpiece of his helmet.

"I have orders to see the Commander," Micah said.

"Show me."

"Verbal orders."

"Not good enough, buddy."

"If I don't get through to him, the Kudite leaders will be angry. Do you want to risk that?"

The soldiers looked at each other. "What harm can he do?" the other one said. "He sure isn't packing any weapons, other than what we can see," he added with a smirk, "and that doesn't look too lethal."

Micah flushed at the insult but said nothing. The taller one shrugged and stepped aside to let him pass.

When he reached the end of the hall and turned right, he came face to face with Royal.

"Oh god, Micah! I was beginning to think I had dreamed the whole thing!" Royal clasped his arms around Micah tightly. "I was so sure you must be dead!"

Micah swayed, his mind a sudden tumble of emotions. A flash of the old yearning, brought on by that familiar spicy smell, almost made him forget himself.

"I thought you were dead, too," he said weakly.

"I never would have left you after the crash if I'd even guessed you might be still alive!" Royal went on. "I've been waiting for hours. Come in here. Harlon's letting me use the room next to his tonight. God, you look wonderful!" He pushed Micah inside the room and stepped back to look at him again. "Take off that barbaric collar thing. I've got a uniform here for you and a sniper car on the roof outside. Hurry! And braid your hair. Will that blue band on your forehead come off?"

"Wait!" Micah backed away, confused. "What are you talking about, Royal?"

"Rescuing you, of course! The Commander and I have been talking about you ever since dinner. It's risky, but you're a Terran citizen after all and —"

"No! I don't want to be rescued. Not this time."

"What the hell are you talking about?"

"You apparently had your chance after the crash, is that

what you're saying? Well now, Royal, it's too late!"

"Don't be pig headed! I saw what that barbarian did to you tonight. He hurt you!"

"And you burned your initials into my ass with a heat rod."

"For god's sake, Micah! That was different!"

"Was it?"

Royal punched a clenched fist into his hand in exasperation. "What have they done to you?" he asked.

"Attlad has given me what I have been looking for all my life. I just didn't know what it was."

"You can stand there, naked and oiled and painted like some…some alien harlot, and you tell me you don't want to come back to me? To us? You prefer this life of shame?"

"I don't see it that way."

"Christ!" Royal paced over to the window and back again. "It's the accident! It damaged your brain. That's it, isn't it?"

"There's nothing wrong with my brain, Royal." Micah smiled. Royal always needed a concrete reason for everything that went against what he wanted to believe.

"But Micah, I'm giving you a choice, don't you see?"

"I had a choice. I escaped with my friend Forrest. I chose to go back and he went on alone."

"Forrest Mason, you mean? He didn't get far, Micah. They killed him." Micah shivered. "Your friends the Kudites killed him when he was almost home. They left him at the edge of the desert with a spear through his heart for our scouts to find. You call that a choice?"

"I didn't know that. Nevertheless, my choice was valid."

"Oh for god's sake, Micah, you're a Nebula Warrior, like I am. How can you let them degrade you like this?" He gestured to the rings, to the chain on his burnished chest.

Micah stepped closer, suddenly angry with this man

who refused to see how things really were, how they had been between them. "It's what you always wanted to do with me, but you never had the nerve! You were too concerned about what other people would think, if they found out!"

"What are you babbling about?"

"Did you ever wonder why we were paired, Royal? Did you ever stop to question that? To analyze what it was about us that should have worked?"

"It did work! It would again if you'd just come back!"

"No. You don't have the strength to be true to your own feelings and desires. You never would. You didn't even have the courage to put your mark where it might be seen on me. You had to try and hide it."

Royal stared at him in disbelief.

"No," Micah went on. "what we had was a fantasy. What I have with Attlad is real."

"Why, you're nothing but an exhibitionist," Royal spluttered at last, "a sex toy for that perverted alien."

Micah shook back his hair. "This isn't getting us anywhere," he said. "I must go."

"You're a fool!" Royal said. "Do you think Harlon wants you?"

"What he wants is not the point," Micah said. He opened the door and went out.

It was strange how little he felt moved by the fact that his lover was still alive. Perhaps if he hadn't seen him just now, if Royal hadn't had the chance to show his true colors, he might have grieved. Not now. He knocked on the door and went inside.

The Commander was wearing a wine colored dressing gown. He smiled broadly at Micah and came towards him holding out his hand. "Sub-Captain Micah Starion! Royal filled me in on your story. We'll help any way we can."

Micah shook his hand politely. "Thank you for the welcome, sir. But my name is Chento, now. My master sent me to you for the night."

There was a sudden deep silence in the room. Harlon turned and went back to the comfortable arm chair by the artificial fire and sat down heavily. "I don't understand," he said. "Didn't you talk to Royal?"

"Yes, sir. I'm afraid he doesn't understand my choice of a new life."

"That's hardly surprising," murmured the Commander. He ran a tired hand over his face. "Look, Starion, you have a fine record with Terrafleet Corps, and can look forward to a bright future. Are you sure you want to throw this all away to live as a slave? With these...barbarians?"

"I have made my decision, sir."

"Royal is a fine man. He has been my E.A. for about four months, now. He can't fly any more, you know. He lost his nerve after the accident. It would mean a lot to him if you would come back."

"I'm sorry, but no," Micah said. He resented what the Commander was trying to do, even though he understood it.

"There's a robe in the cupboard. Would you mind putting it on?"

"I will do whatever you order, sir." Micah retrieved the robe and put it on.

"There. That's better. Sit down, sit down." Harlon looked relieved that Micah was clothed, at least partially. "You know, Starion, I'm very concerned about you. I've heard so much about you from Royal, I feel I know you."

Micah was sitting in the armchair opposite him, watching him intently, the way he did Attlad, watching for signals, signs, changes of expression. "Royal didn't really know me, sir," he said softly.

"Perhaps not." Harlon steepled his fingers. "I sometimes

wonder if it's possible for one person to really know another. In a way, I envoy your Attlad. He doesn't have to know you, only himself, and his own desires."

"On the surface, that's true," Micah said. "But that is only a superficial assessment. The bond between master and slave is very complex. A master must know his slave thoroughly for it to work on all levels. That's the reason for the tests a Personal Body Slave must go through with the Kudites. And you forget, sir, that I made the final choice. I went back to Attlad."

"You didn't chose to be here."

"I chose to want what my master wants. Therefore, I did chose to be here."

Harlon laughed, throwing back his head in real amusement. "You're a tonic," he said. "In this job, there isn't much to laugh about."

"I can help you forget." Micah got to his feet and went and knelt between the man's knees. He laid his hands on the commander's hard narrow thighs. "You're very tense."

"It comes with the territory."

"I'll get you a drink." Micah went to the sideboard and poured a glass of the heady elixir he found there. He brought the bottle back with him and handed the glass to Harlon. "Tell me about your job. There must be some good points."

"You don't really want to hear about that," Harlon said, but he began to talk. Soon he had veered away from problems at the Base and on to personal things, haltingly at first, then picking up speed, like a man who hasn't had anyone to talk to for a long time.

As the commander talked, Micah kept refilling the glass, and all the time, his complete attention was focused on the older man. Harlon was beginning to relax.

After a while, Micah ran his hand up under the robe.

"Wait." Harlon went to the door and locked it. "If you're going to stay, I don't want anyone walking in on us." He sat down again, his knees spread casually, almost inviting Micah's hands. He finished off his wine and signalled for another. "So, you are my slave for the night."

"Yes, sir."

"Let's see if I can think of a better use for you than pouring me wine. Go over to that chest of drawers and open the second drawer on the right. The combination is 330." Micah did as he was told and looked down at the black lace and gauze inside. He felt an unpleasant jolt in the pit of his stomach. "Take out a pair of panties and put them on," Harlon went on. "Then put on the full length black lace peignoir beside it."

Micah studied the lace bikinis intently and at last, forced himself to step into them. They were tight. It was hard to stuff his cock inside and the lacy string at the back cut into the crack of his ass, rubbing against his anus as he moved. It was about the most erotic thing he had ever had on.

"Now the bra," Harlon said.

The cups of the black lace bra were full, padded with a substance that moved under the hand. When Micah finally got it on, the effect was alarming. He glanced at Harlon.

"You're doing fine. The garter belt, next."

Micah looked uncertainly into the drawer, not even sure what he was looking for. He withdrew another piece of black lace, with long black garters dangling from it. When it was fastened, it hung low on his hips, leaving a wide band of bronzed skin before the lace of the bikinis began. Without being told, he took a pair of black nylon stockings out of the drawer and sat down on the chair to put them on.

Micah felt the hot flush in his cheeks as he struggled with the stockings under Harlon's constant gaze. He had lost all control of the situation which five minutes earlier he had felt so confident about guiding. Now, his anxiety was rising, and with it, fear. Suddenly he was afraid of this man, who just a few moments ago had seemed to warm, so reasonable, so caring. Micah had no clear idea what was expected from him now, and it frightened him in a way his master's most painful demands never had.

When he had finally fastened the stockings, he stood up and struggled awkwardly into the peignoir. It had long full sleeves and a voluminous skirt and it tied around the waist with a sash. It felt very odd where it touched his skin and brushed against his nylon covered legs. He was very aware that it was practically transparent.

Harlon was coming towards him, smiling, but Micah no longer trusted the smile. He looked into the drawer and pulled out a sting of pearls which he hung around Micah's neck.

"Beautiful," he said softly. "Now, the heels." He opened another drawer and displayed a long row of high heeled shoes in varying large sizes. They were all black, shiny and dangerous looking. "Something there will fit you."

After a few tries, Micah found a pair he could get into, but walking in them was torture. His toes were crushed together, his balance was thrown off by the high heels, his ankles wobbled dangerously. He was like a child learning to walk all over again. Micah wasn't used to feeling awkward. He blushed furiously as Harlon laughed at his efforts.

"You must learn grace, my dear," Harlon said, taking a silver wand from the drawer. "But first, sit down and let's fix your hair a bit. It's far too wild."

Micah sat down on the bench in front of the mirror, and Harlon rubbed cream into his hair and brushed it around his fingers into a semblance of ringlets. Then he pinned a ribbon around it so that the blue and gold band on his forehead was completely covered. The ribbon was tied in a bow on one side and the ends hung turn over one ear, tickling his cheek.

"Put on the lipstick," Harlon said, "and then you will be ready for your lessons."

"Yes, sir."

"Yes, daddy."

"Yes, daddy." Chilled, Micah picked up the lipstick, opened it, outlined his lips. The face that looked back, frightened him. He would not have thought it possible to eradicate his masculinity to this extent. It was still there, but muted, blurred. He was a warrior! He had endured great pain and suffering for his master. But could he subdue his own macho pride? His hand shook as he put down the lipstick.

When he was ready, Harlon ordered him to practice walking. He opened all the doors of the apartment, revealing a long stretch from the front sitting room, down a hall past his private office, the bathroom and onto the bedroom beyond.

"Walk right to the windows, then turn and come back. And swing your hips, there's a good girl. Keep your head up. Be graceful."

Micah felt anything but graceful as he tried to follow Harlon's commands. He felt like a caricature of a hooker in some ancient movie. He would just master the hip swinging, when his ankle would turn, throwing him off. When he recovered and concentrated on balancing in the killer shoes, he would forget to swing his hips.

Harlon announced that he was not pleased. "You have one more chance," he said.

And Micah set off on the long walk again. But again he turned his ankle, wincing with the pain. Twice.

"You are recalcitrant," Harlon remarked. He picked up

a leather belt from the chair. "Hold out your hands."

Micah did what he was told and gritted his teeth as the leather stung his palms. Harlon concentrated on one, then the other, until they were both red and sore. "Do it again," he commanded.

Micah turned and walked away. He tried to remember the women he had seen tonight, but they were all in uniform and none of them would ever move their asses the way he was being forced to do. Forget reality, he told himself. This is Harlon's fantasy. Give him what he wants.

But it was hard to understand what, exactly, the man did want. Once Micah was able to walk without stumbling, and was beginning to feel a little more confident, Harlon made him move faster.

"That's enough strolling," he said. "Now I want speed."

To make sure he got it, Harlon moved along behind him, urging him forward first with words, then with electric jolts from his silver wand. Micah's calves were aching by now, his feet hurt, and both ankles were sore from the twisting he had given them. Then, to make things worse, he tripped on the long skirt.

When he got back to his feet, Harlon sat down on the bed. "You will be punished for that," he said. "Bend over my knee and pull your dress up."

Micah obeyed. Shame almost overcame him as he knelt and tried to pull up the skirt and bend over the commander's knee at the same time. It was so awkward. Harlon let him struggle until he was in place, then pulled the black chiffon skirts up until they covered his head, exposing his buttocks and the black lace and the garters.

Micah tensed for the pain. Nothing happened. "Sweet little ass," murmured Harlon, and he began to caress it with a feather. Micah jerked. The feather trailed along the crack of his ass, between his legs. He could feel it caress his balls though the flimsy nylon. He jerked again, unable to control the reaction of his muscles. "You will learn grace. You will learn control," Harlon said. Then he touched one buttock with the silver wand and a shock went through Micah, contorting his body so that it jumped almost off Harlon's knees.

The commander laughed. "Enough playing," he said. Then he paused for a moment to pick up a long ruler that was lying on the table. He began to beat Micah's buttocks, swinging his arm high to get more force to the blows. It went on and on. Try as he might, Micah couldn't keep back the tears and at last he sobbed openly. That seemed to satisfy the commander.

"Stand up. I want to check your control."

When Micah stood before him, tearful, red faced and shaking, Harlon opened the lace skirt and told Micah to hold it back so he could see his crotch. He touched the feather to the black lace covering Micah's cock. Standing with his legs apart in the high heeled shoes, his buttocks swollen and burning, Micah twitched reflexively. His cock began to stiffen at last under the constant teasing, thrusting its way out past the lace. Harlon pulled down the panties, releasing it and continued to torment it, stroking it with the feather up and down, on top, underneath. Micah began to shake.

"Sir, I can't…"

"Yes, you can." He withdrew the feather for a moment, then started again. Micah began thrusting his hips forward, trying to gain some release from the insubstantial feather which was withdrawn every time he was close to achieving orgasm. At last, Harlon seemed to tire of the game. He picked up a glass from the table, held it over the head of Micah's penis and ordered him to come. As Harlon touched his cock, Micah involuntarily obeyed, the spasm almost making him lose his balance. Harlon laughed.

"Now, let's see if you have learned anything."

Micah tucked his cock back in place and readjusted the dress. Once again he paraded up and down in front of Harlon, swinging his hips, shortening his stride, trying to walk with one foot in front of the other. He was improving, but pain was now shooting up through his calves and thighs. Every step stretched the elastic of the garters across his sore buttocks and his feet, cramped in the narrow shoes, were giving him real agony.

At last, Harlon announced that it was time to go to bed. To his dismay, Micah discovered he was expected to sleep in full regalia. At least he could take off the shoes! He had never felt such blessed relief as when he took off the accursed things and lay back in the bed. Harlon lay down beside him. He was naked, his body hard and muscular, in spite of the grey hair and the ropy blue veins in his legs. He took Micah in his arms, caressed his long ringlets, kissed the lipstick off his mouth. He lay on top of the tall athletic slave, pressing himself against the black lace that covered the bulging crotch. Micah closed his eyes.

"Look at me, dammit!"

"Yes, sir." At once, he opened his eyes again, watching beads of perspiration form on the Commander's forehead.

Harlon was panting as he lay between Micah's raised knees, pumping his pale old man's cock against Micah's hard stomach until finally he came. With a deep sigh, the Commander laid his head on the soft lace of the black bra that cut cruelly into Micah's rib cage, and fell asleep, a satisfied smile on his face.

Micah clenched his teeth and thought of his master, the hard dark man who demanded so much of him, who owned him body and soul. Surely this was the ultimate test? This evening when he had been forced to go so much against his own nature? But the evening wasn't over.

Micah waited for a long time before he slid out from under the Commander and got out of bed. Quickly he peeled off the lace and tulle and frilly nylon until his magnificent body was naked again. Then he went into the Commander's private office and closed the door.

The eye of the computer which was never turned off, glowed eerily from the wall, casting menacing shadows in the small room. Micah keyed in his requests quickly and was asked for the password. Of course! He cursed under his breath. The words he tried were long outdated. Then he tried 'daddy'. Nothing. 'Daddy's girl'. No luck. 'Lace'. Bingo! He stared intently at the rows of figures, the comments, the memos as they flashed onto the screen at the request of his flying fingers. He made notes of everything he thought was important, afraid to activate the printer for fear of waking up Harlon. Besides, he knew this machine was hooked into the main data base and there would be a record somewhere of all use. When he was finished, he left everything as he had found it and tiptoed out into the front room.

Here he scooped up the hated lace clothing and put it back in its locked drawer. He had forgotten the shoes, but decided they didn't matter. One thing he kept, the sash of the peignoir which he tied around his head. Under it, were the notes he had made from the computer.

With a last look around the room, Micah unlocked the door and crept out into the early morning hush of the Commander's Residence. It was with a great feeling of satisfaction he turned in the direction of Attlad's quarters.

TWELVE

he two guards were still at their posts in the hall outside the Commander's quarters. One of them gave a low whistle as Micah went by. The other swatted at his naked ass playfully.

"Old Harlon give you a rough time, sweet cheeks?" he whispered.

"Nah. His ass is red like that from hanging out in the open all the time." His companion chuckled.

Their soft mocking laughter followed Micah until he was around the corner. He walked faster, down to the end of the corridor and up the flight of stairs that led to Attlad's room. At the top, Micah opened the door softly and slipped into the darkness.

He paused to get his bearings. Something didn't feel right. Micah tensed, his senses alert to the strangeness around him. A tightness in the air. Strain. He leapt to his right and ducked as an arm came at him. Micah rolled aside, jumped lightly to his feet and connected with a broad shoulder. A man grunted.

"Chento!"

Micah froze, but didn't lessen his grip on the man's head. The scent of the man was familiar. "Attlad!" He released him as the lights came on.

Sar stood by the light switch, laughing softly.

"Master, I am sorry."

Before Micah could kneel, Attlad took his slave by the shoulders and looked at him, deep into his blue eyes. Then he embraced him, his hands running over Micah's shoulders and back, lingering on his sore buttocks. He separated them, caressed his crack, pushed gently inside his anus. It was as if he was repossessing him, inch by inch. And as he did, Micah's cock rose, arcing towards his master hungrily. But Attlad pushed him away and sat down at the table beside Sar.

"Were you successful?" he asked.

Micah took off the sash he had wound around his head, unfolded it and gave the notes to Attlad. "I will translate them for you," he signed.

Attlad nodded and Sar prepared to make notes as he went over the figures, facts, statistics which the computer had divulged.

"Still under," remarked Attlad with satisfaction. "They have no clear idea of our strength and they over stress our weaknesses. Good."

Sar nodded. "Just what we needed to know." He was signing too, a courtesy that Micah acknowledged with a smile. "Just as we suspected, they see only the outward sign of the primitive lifestyle we have chosen. They do not understand."

Attlad snorted his derision. "They will never understand what is different," he said.

"I will leave you, now." Sar stood up and bowed briefly to Attlad. Before he left, he touched Micah and smiled.

"Well done."

Micah signed his thanks.

When Sar was gone, Attlad took a handful of Micah's hair and smelled it. He made a face.

"Come." He pulled him gently into the bath room and undressed himself. He pushed Micah into the shower and covered his body with soap, washing his slave all over, running his strong possessive hands over every inch of Micah's body in an effort to rinse away the Commander's touch. And all the time, he muttered words Micah couldn't understand, although he recognized his own name over and over. Then Attlad washed his hair, not gently like Simon, but roughly, as a man will who is not used to the job, tangling his hands and pulling it often, while Micah bit his lip and tried not to jerk his head away When that ordeal was over, Attlad told him to spread his legs and lean against the tiles. Then he entered him, thrusting upwards with such powerful strokes, Micah was lifted off his feet and reached for the shower rod to keep from falling. He was impaled, filled completely by his master's swollen desire. The warm water beat down on them, and Micah opened his mouth to it as his hair flowed down his back in a heavy river and twined onto Attlad's straining nakedness. Then Attlad reached around and brought him to ecstasy with his soapy hands. Weak and exhausted, they sank together to the floor and sat entwined as the shower of rain poured down on them. Attlad laughed, holding him close in his strong arms.

"It will overflow," Micah pointed out. "We are sitting on the outlet."

Attlad reached up and turned off the water. Then he leaned over and kissed him. "Come to bed," he said. "It is almost morning."

"We will go back to the Complex tomorrow?" Micah asked, climbing onto the bed. He felt that he was not really safe on the Base.

"Tomorrow we sign the treaty. Then, we must go to the Citadel." Attlad gathered his pliant slave into his arms and held him against his chest. Micah moved his hips, willing himself to open wide for his master. He sighed as he felt Attlad's thick cock slip into him. Attlad's hand played with his right nipple ring.

"You have passed every test, my love slave," he said. "But there is still the Citadel."

Micah sighed and closed his eyes.

Tomorrow came quickly. Micah tottered with exhaustion. His head was aching. The muscles in his calves and thighs still hurt from the night before, and there were red welts on his ass from Harlon's beating. Even his eyes were tired and gritty. But he ate his breakfast, brought to him in a bowl on Attlad's instructions, put on his collar, and followed his master to the treaty signing.

The Commander looked right through him. He spoke to Attlad and to Sar, smiling at them as he waited for the formal words to be translated. He signed his name, handed the ceremonial pen for them to mark their symbol. Micah knelt by Attlad's side and swayed with fatigue. When it was time to go, Attlad pulled on the leash to rouse him. It took all his self-control to force himself to walk out of the Commander's residence onto the moving sidewalk. Just before the official party was out of sight, he caught a glimpse of Royal, standing at a window looking down at the departing group. His face was angry, bitter. He refused to meet Micah's eye.

When they reached the horse, Attlad scooped him up in front of him and rode quickly back to the carrier, holding Micah against him all the way so he wouldn't fall. It was a great relief to ride onto the carrier and see the huge ramp close behind them with a clang.

Attlad slipped to the floor and pulled Micah into his arms.

"It is over," Micah signed, his fingers light against his master's muscled chest.

Attlad shook his head. "It is only the beginning. Ahead there lies the Citadel."

The Citadel
by Kyle Stone

The dark, dangerous sequel to the mesmerizing *Initiation of P.B 500*.

Having proven himself worthy of his stunning master, Micah—now known only by the number '500'—faces new challenges. The Citadel is not like the hard world of the warrior. Here treachery lurks as he enters its seductive portals—alone. Will he survive this brutal and terrifying test? Will he ever see his master again?

††   gay sf/sm adventure ~ erotica

MEN *agerie*
stories of passion and dark fantasy
by Kyle Stone

The latest collection of dark erotic stories from the master. *MENagerie* takes us on a breathless, mind-bending exploration of desire and gay fantasy.

"Stone has the ability to produce erotica that not only creates a stir in your shorts but also makes you think about your own fantasies, relationships and your identity as a sexual gay man.... Stone is truly one of the best authors of gay erotica today." Unzipped Magazine

††   gay erotica

Printed in the United States
77710LV00001B/104

9 780968 677636